"Stop looking at me like that," Leslie ordered Joe with great bravado.

"Why? Do I make you nervous?" he asked, enjoying himself.

"A little," she admitted, tilting her chin defiantly.

"Look, lady," he said, merriment in his voice, "I can't remember the time I jumped an unwilling or unconscious woman. I didn't give in to the temptation to peek inside your dress after you fainted, even though you've provoked me ever since you ran me off the road. I haven't attacked you yet. I promise you, you're safe with me. Now, do you want me to zip you up or not?"

"Yes," she said, taking up his challenge.

"Please," he reminded her good-naturedly.

"Yes, please," she ground out through clenched teeth.

His hand brushed the ruffles of her skirt, then reached around her waist to pull her close to him. Leslie stood stunned and breathless in his arms.

"Maybe I shouldn't have made such a hasty promise," he said, and lowered his mouth to hers. . . .

WHAT ARE *LOVESWEPT* ROMANCES?

They are stories of true romance and touching emotion. We believe those two very important ingredients are constants in our highly sensual and very believable stories in the *LOVESWEPT* line. Our goal is to give you, the reader, stories of consistently high quality that may sometimes make you laugh, sometimes make you cry, but are always fresh and creative and contain many delightful surprises within their pages.

Most romance fans read an enormous number of books. Those they truly love, they keep. Others may be traded with friends and soon forgotten. We hope that each *LOVESWEPT* romance will be a treasure—a "keeper." We will always try to publish

LOVE STORIES YOU'LL NEVER FORGET
BY AUTHORS YOU'LL ALWAYS REMEMBER

The Editors

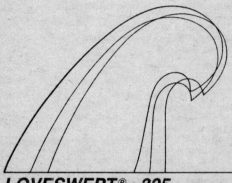

LOVESWEPT® · 325

Mary Kay McComas
Bound to Happen

 BANTAM BOOKS
TORONTO · NEW YORK · LONDON · SYDNEY · AUCKLAND

*For those so loved, they feel
they can take love for granted.*

One

"What did I say?" Leslie asked, holding her hands out, bewildered.

"That's exactly what I want to know," her mother said, brushing past her, angry and frustrated. She rattled the knob on the bathroom door, casting Leslie an exasperated glare. Finally, in a too-calm voice she called, "Beth? Beth, honey, open the door. It's Mom, honey. You can come out now."

A mournful wail came from the bathroom, and once again, Leslie felt her mother's gaze on her.

"Lord, Leslie, what have you done now?" the older woman asked.

"Nothing. One minute we were just having a little talk, and the next thing I knew, she was crying and running into the bathroom, locking the door behind her."

"Well, what on earth were you talking about?"

"Nothing much," Leslie said thoughtfully, going back over the conversation in her mind. "I was asking her how she knew Paul was the right man to marry."

Mrs. Rothe groaned wearily. "And you couldn't have asked her that question six months ago? Before we invited the Senators, and before we ordered the three hundred pounds of shrimp?"

"To be truthful, I didn't really think she'd get this far. I—"

"Leslie, don't be truthful. Lie. I've told you a hundred times, total honesty is not the virtue it's cracked up to be," Mrs. Rothe said, her voice dripping with sarcasm. "Really. I'm surprised that in all these years you've never heard of tact or diplomacy."

Leslie sighed in dejection. It was the same old story. She'd ask Beth a simple question, Beth would end up in hysterics, and somehow it was always Leslie's fault. Was it her fault Beth was an emotional flake?

"Beth, honey," her mother called again. "Please come out. Leslie didn't mean anything by grilling you. You know how she is . . ."

"I didn't grill her," Leslie muttered in a low voice.

Her mother had once commented that if Leslie had half of Beth's feelings and Beth had half of Leslie's brains and spirit, she would have two normal daughters. As it was, she had one with no feelings and one with no brains.

Leslie hadn't appreciated the comparison. She had just as many feelings as Beth. She simply didn't let them hang out like her sister did. She kept them safe and sheltered and didn't waste them on little things, like every other man who walked by.

As for Beth being brainless, well, at times like this, that charge was a little hard to argue with, Leslie admitted to herself.

"What's going on in here?" Leslie's father asked from the doorway of the vestibule. "The guests are getting antsy."

Leslie and her mother exchanged looks. Mrs. Rothe spoke first. "It's my fault, Stan. I lost my mind for a couple of minutes and left the girls alone in the same room. Now Beth's locked herself in the bathroom, and all she keeps saying is, There's more to it than love."

Stan Rothe frowned in confusion and moved into the room. "More to what than love?"

"Marriage, I suppose. That is what you were grilling her about, wasn't it?" Leslie's mother asked, turning the focus of guilt on her older daughter.

Leslie nodded, then looked at her father and shrugged helplessly. Of all the people in the world he seemed to understand her best. He winked at Leslie sympathetically and patted her shoulder.

"It's a little like the dinosaur question, honey," he said under his breath for only Leslie to hear. For years now, he'd been using that example to let Leslie know that some questions didn't have factual answers. There had been dinosaurs, their bones were the proof. But nobody knows what they *really* looked like or where they went. Leslie had to accept that they were there once and let someone else drive themselves nuts with how they looked and what happened to them. In essence he was telling Leslie not to toil too hard over the questions of love and marriage, because they just existed with no tangible or logical facts to support them.

He moved on to copy his wife's actions by first rattling the door knob, then calling through the bathroom door. "Bethy. It's Dad. Unlock the door and come out now. If you've changed your mind about the wedding, we'll work it out. If you're just confused, we'll talk. But we can't settle anything if you stay in there."

"Leslie says love isn't enough. It's an emotion that can be easily mistaken for simple lust, which isn't love at all," Beth said rather tearfully from the other side of the door. "What if I'm just feeling lust?"

"Then you won't have a dull honeymoon," her father said, more to himself than his daughter. But after a not so playful whack on the arm from his wife, he called, "Beth, you know in your heart what you're feeling. Haven't I always told you to listen to your heart? And that if you did, it would always make the wisest decisions for you?"

Beth sniffed loudly. "Yes."

"So, what is it telling you?"

"It says I love Paul. I'll die without him."

Leslie threw up her hands in defeat. Even Beth's wise old heart was overly dramatic. No wonder the poor girl couldn't think straight.

"Good," Stan Rothe said. "Then come on out and let's have a wedding."

"No."

"Why not?"

"Leslie isn't stupid. You say so all the time. If she says there has to be more to it than just love, then there probably is. I have to have at least two real reasons for marrying Paul."

Mr. and Mrs. Rothe grimaced and glared at Leslie. Again a dejected sigh escaped her. Would she ever learn to stop talking to her poor brainless sister, she wondered with self-derision.

"No, Beth. You don't need two real reasons. You need to listen to your heart. In fact, Leslie was so upset at having upset you, she left," her father was telling the bride to be, his eyes pleading with the maid of honor for understanding—and a hasty departure. Leslie nodded and turned to go. "Leslie wanted me to be sure and tell you that she thinks Paul is the right man for you and . . ."

Leslie moved out into the hall, the door closing softly behind her. The anger and self-disgust she was feeling made her heartsick. She had wanted answers to her questions, she needed them. But she should have known better than to try and get them from Beth. Not that Beth hadn't tried to help her. To the best of her ability she'd tried.

But Beth couldn't give definite examples of the

ways in which Paul made her "feel good." She couldn't give exact reasons why she would trust Paul with her life or trust him to be faithful to her. What had Paul done to deserve such faith? In the end Beth had become so frustrated trying to explain that she'd begun doubting herself. The added doubts combined with the normal nervousness of a bride had turned Beth into a basket case. And it *was* Leslie's fault. She should have known better. She'd been dealing with her sister for twenty-three years and hadn't gotten one logical answer from her yet.

Once in the parking lot, Leslie suddenly realized she'd forgotten to change out of her gown. It was a hideous affair with a low-cut bodice and bell-shaped skirt that was so like Beth and so unlike herself, she could hardly stand looking at it. And what was Beth going to do for a maid of honor, she wondered.

She turned to retrace her steps, then changed her mind. Her mother would handle it. She'd substitute a bride's maid for Leslie, and no one would be the wiser—if the wedding actually took place at all. And Leslie certainly didn't want to go back in there to change clothes. She could change at home and leave it to her mother to retrieve the clothes she'd worn to the church that morning.

She was in the process of wadding the hoop and voluminous skirt into something she could sit on, when she heard the church door open and close behind her.

Her mother approached, her gown swishing louder than her footsteps in the silence between them. Without hesitation, she took Leslie's face between her hands and came eye to eye with her eldest daughter.

"For what it's worth," she said, "I know you didn't intend for this to happen."

"I'm really sorry."

"I know, honey. And I'd rather you didn't leave,

but it might be for the best. Beth has always looked up to you and admired you so. She thinks you have all the answers to everything." Eve Rothe smiled sympathetically at her daughter. "She'd be surprised if she stopped to realize you were coming to her for an answer this time, wouldn't she?"

Leslie grinned back at her mother self-consciously. "Yeah."

"When it happens to you, dear—and it's bound to happen—you won't be able to explain it any better than Beth could. Try not to let that interfere with it, though. Love has no rhyme or reason. It just is."

Leslie nodded to pacify her mother, but she still didn't understand. How could the whole world make such a big deal out of something so . . . unreal? Air, vapor, radio waves . . . there were lots of things that couldn't be seen, touched, smelled, or heard and still had perfectly good explanations behind them. Why didn't love? And how did you find it if you didn't know anything about it?

"Are you still going to take your vacation?" her mother asked.

"Yes. I was tired before all this. Now I really need it," Leslie said, again gathering the skirt, trying to decide the best way to get it into her Volvo, finally deciding to just hike up the gown and sit flat on the seat. Pushing the skirt down around her, she looked up to see that her mother had moved up beside the car door.

"Well, try not to dwell on this. I think you've learned your lesson. And I'm sure your father will be able to talk her out of the bathroom soon. It'll work out. You go. Rest up. And come back as your old sweet self. You've been working too hard lately. Lighten up. Have a little fun."

"Okay, Mom," Leslie agreed halfheartedly as she kissed her mother's cheek. "I'll try."

•   •   •

Depressed, disgruntled, and feeling disgraced by her part in the disastrous prenuptial incident with Beth, Leslie took the freeway on her way home.

It was a clear, warm midsummer Saturday in Denver. The car windows were down, and the wind whipped at her hair. The Rockies rose tall and majestic in the distance. The jagged blue mountain line seemed to rise up and join with the cloudless blue of the sky like one continuous curtain marking the end of the earth, one part so solid, the other so empty and yet so perfect and complete.

For Leslie there was something ethereal and soothing about the scene before her. It's agelessness, the way it never changed, made her life seem simple and at the same time, valuable. The mountains called out to her and lifted her spirits. She suddenly was glad to be alive, to be able to feel the heat of the sun on her skin and the wind in her hair.

The events at the church and her doubts and loneliness slowly slipped away as she kept driving, heading straight for the mountains. She saw the exit she needed to take to get home and watched it slip by. Normally not an impulsive person, she rarely was taken by whims. But this time, the impulse was too strong and seemed so right.

Oh, she knew somewhere in the back of her mind that if she were adamant about going to the mountains, she should go home first and maybe eat something—and definitely change her clothes—but this whim knew her too well. It knew that if it allowed Leslie to stop for anything practical or level-headed, she would come to her senses and nip it in the bud. So it took advantage of her weakened state of mind and gained full control.

In less than an hour she'd passed through the town of Bailey, her destination firmly set in her mind. As the data-research analyst for a large property-development company, Leslie had been studying a particular parcel of land deep inside the Gunnison National Forest as a site for a proposed ski resort. Unfortunately, it hadn't been her only project. For months now, she'd been running herself ragged preparing proposals for projects in locations all over the Rocky Mountain states. And she never had the time to actually see the proposal sites.

It wasn't necessary for her to see them in person. The maps, the geological studies, national park records, and a multitude of other surveys and reports were all indicators she used to determine whether to recommend or reject a particular site. The one she was heading for had all the earmarks of being an excellent location for a winter playground for the elite. Leslie had wanted to see the before and after of a new project, and this one was of particular interest to her because of the considerable uproar environmental groups had caused throughout the planning.

And so to give the left side of her brain a sense of maintaining its equilibrium during this escapade, Leslie went the extra distance to Buena Vista and without any trouble found the deserted logging road which would take her into the isolated mountains.

Not only was Leslie dressed inappropriately for the journey, but her Volvo didn't seem to be appreciating what was being passed off as a road beneath its wheels. The grade was so steep that the car's transmission wouldn't get out of first gear even though the motor raced powerfully to pull it ahead. The Volvo bounced, tilted, and swayed as it moved over bumps and in and out of potholes. Still Leslie pushed on. She'd come too far to turn back, and the downhill trip would be much easier. She even promised the Volvo a tune-up and overhaul at the foreign auto repair shop of its choice if it would just hang in there with her.

As she drove higher and higher, she was forced to roll up the car windows against the chilly air and let the sun warm the interior of the car. When at last she came to a basin where she saw evidence of an old mining camp, she instinctively recognized the area as her destination. She pulled in beside one of the two dilapidated old buildings that remained, but when she attempted to get out to stretch her legs, the cold wind blew gooseflesh across her bare shoulders and arms, and Leslie decided to remain inside the car.

She could see all she wanted to from where she was. A miniature model of the project had been constructed for the investors, and it took very little imagination for her to picture how it would look once completed. She could see the summit lodge high above her. She knew where each ski run would be cut through the dense ponderosa pines, spruce, and aspens. And there, not far from where she sat, would be the base with its posh lodgelike hotel. More of the land would be cleared for shops and restaurants to keep the not so serious skiers happy. And . . .

Leslie sighed heavily. Her job notwithstanding, what was about to happen to the beautiful mountain was almost sacrilegious, a crying shame at the very least. Her heart sank. She'd come all this way, full of hope and a sense of her own being, to look at something that wouldn't even exist in two years' time.

It was as if the mountain had called out to her saying, Come see me now, because I'll never be this beautiful again. It was as if an inner voice was telling her to start really living, because even the mountains wouldn't last forever.

Feeling nearly as terrible as she had when she first left the church some four hours earlier, Leslie started the downhill journey home.

She became preoccupied with her thoughts and ambivalent to the spectacular view that spread itself before her in a panoramic vista of fierce, rugged mountaintops and gentle, wooded slopes and valleys. The wealthy patrons who no doubt would flock to the new ski resort would certainly get their money's worth in view, Leslie finally decided as she traveled down the center of the old dirt road, hoping to miss as many holes as possible.

She kept trying to shake the overwhelming feeling of isolation and aloneness that threatened to engulf her and blurred her eyes with tears, but it stuck tenaciously and grew. In the recesses of her mind she began to wonder what was wrong with her. She'd never been an overly emotional person. She'd never felt so sorry for herself or so dissatisfied with her life before. Since when did she care what a project did to the natural beauty of the land? She'd always thought the developments had a beauty of their own. Why had she been so disappointed that Beth hadn't been able to answer her questions about love and the rightness of having one particular man in your life as opposed to any other man? What difference did it make anyway? She had her career and plenty of friends, and led an active, productive life. What else mattered?

From out of nowhere a large truck loomed up directly in front of her. She could see her own expression of shocked surprise reflected in the driver's face. With no time to consider her options, Leslie's instincts took over. She jerked the steering wheel to the right. There was a brief blur of green and brown and blue before her eyes closed.

The next thing to register in Leslie's brain was the

absolute and total dead silence. Then came the sound of her own breathing, loud, deep, and uneven. She felt nothing but the painful beating of her heart. Gradually other sensations returned. Her tense muscles unwound to a tingling, liquid state. Her eyes opened but remained unseeing. Slowly they focused and began feeding data to her brain.

She wasn't dead. Nor was she injured badly. She ached all over and would have a few bruises, but she was most certainly in one piece and mobile.

Her car was facing downward into a steep but shallow ravine, lodged forcefully against a large boulder. The hood and front end of the car were grossly distorted and damaged. Before she could mourn the loss of her car and realize that she was now stranded in the mountains, thoughts of the other driver flashed into her mind with a panic.

There was a quick loud thump on the window near her face, and Leslie jumped. Turning, she recognized the face she'd seen in the brief seconds before all had been lost to her. There was shock, anger, and a great deal of anxiety in the man's face as he motioned for her to get out of the car.

Leslie pulled on the door handle but without reward. She pulled again and pushed with her shoulder to try and dislodge whatever was keeping the door in place.

The man thumped the window again and indicated in a muffled voice that he wanted her to unlock the back door. Aching and hindered by the hoop and the volumes of material of her dress, Leslie finally managed to unlock the door. The man jerked it open immediately.

"Get out," he ordered in a deep, terse voice.

"Is the car on fire?" Leslie asked, terrorized by the urgency in his voice.

"How the hell should I know? Get out," he ordered

again, his sharpness almost as frightening to Leslie as the thought of being trapped in her car and having the gas tank explode.

Without a thought for modesty or decorum, Leslie laboriously climbed head first into the back seat. She had intended to keep on crawling right out the door to safety but was stunned once again when the man reached in, grabbed her under the arms, and pulled her out of the car. He swore colorfully when the hoops in her skirt caught in the door. Leslie automatically grabbed at her bodice as she felt the man preparing to give one last hoop-snapping tug.

Leslie broke free of the car with such force that the impact of her body hitting his caused him to stagger backward and stumble, taking Leslie with him. Together they rolled the short distance to the bottom of the ravine and came to a stop with the man atop Leslie. Both were breathless from their exertion and the unfortunate results of the near collision moments earlier. After several moments, the man rose up and looked down at Leslie.

He had very dark green eyes that were quick and comprehensive in their detailed inspection of her face and upper chest. His hair was thick and dark, and his sun-bronzed skin was filmed with a fine layer of perspiration.

For long moments he looked at Leslie as if he didn't know what she was or what she was good for. Leslie, on the other hand, was in shock, she decided, as she lay under the stranger, her breath coming in short little gasps, her pulse racing, her skin burning where his body touched hers. She allowed herself a few moments to familiarize herself with the deeply penetrating and highly rapturous feelings being so close to this man stirred in her.

Androgen overload, she finally concluded in her own Leslielike way. It was the only explanation she could come up with that would put her reactions to him into perspective. He certainly wasn't the first handsome man she'd ever seen, but he definitely was the most . . . male. He possessed more of whatever it was that made a man the male of the species than any other person she'd ever met.

'It wasn't just his dark, attractive features or the keenness of his eyes or even the way his broad, muscled shoulders loomed above her, blocking out the midafternoon sun. Whatever it was that masculinized this man so strongly hung in the air about him, grew in every cell of his body, and was as natural to him as the beating of his heart.

"Are you okay?" he asked.

"Yes. Yes, I'm fine," she said, her voice barely a whisper. Leslie found it was very difficult to breathe and talk with a man on her chest.

She watched as his eyes lost their stupefied wonder and grew stormy with his reaction to the reality of the situation. This time his gaze raked over her face and bare shoulders from a different perspective, and Leslie didn't like it at all. She felt defensive before he opened his mouth to speak.

"I hope you have a damned good explanation for all this, lady."

Leslie stared at him wide-eyed and openmouthed for several seconds, temporarily speechless at the man's gall.

"I . . . me? I need an explanation? You've got a lot of nerve," Leslie told him, pushing at his shoulders to free herself. "You weren't an innocent bystander to all this, you know."

The man didn't seem to be willing to give up his superior position. He kept Leslie pinned beneath him. "Well, I sure as hell wasn't the one driving down the middle of the road rubbernecking at all the scenery either."

"That road is supposed to be abandoned. How was I to know you'd be on it?" Leslie asked, making another attempt at getting him to move away from her.

"Abandoned doesn't mean totally forgotten or unusable. What if I'd been some guy with his wife and a trailer full of kids on a camping trip?"

"Then I'd make a citizen's arrest, because this is a restricted area and campers aren't allowed," Leslie said, feeling very proud of herself for remembering that fact, enjoying the wary look that came to the man's face. "Come to think of it," she added bravely, "Just exactly what *are* you doing up here?"

"You're in that getup, and you've been driving around in that car, and you think *I* don't belong up here?" he asked, his expression telling her precisely where he thought she really did belong; his short chuckle mocking her bravado.

Indignant because she knew how foolish she must look to him, Leslie assumed her most disdainful manner and spoke accordingly. "Not that it's any of your concern, but I do happen to have my own reasons for being here like this."

"Oh, this oughta be good," he said, and then laughed as if he were about to hear an old joke once again.

"But I haven't the slightest intention of telling you. Now let me up," she said, growing angry with his impossible attitude.

"That's typical," the man said, moving aside to free Leslie. "Women always clam up when things start to get interesting. It's their way of winning an argument by default. But the fact remains, lady. I look like I belong here a lot more than you do."

"So what?" Leslie groaned, irritated beyond words as she pushed herself into a sitting position. She batted the skirt down when it rose up to meet her, and said, "Accusing each other and arguing about it isn't going to get us anywhere."

"Neither are the vehicles that got us here," the man pointed out.

"Oh, no. Is your truck as badly damaged as my car?" she asked as she scrambled clumsily to her feet.

"Not quite, but it's wedged between two trees, and it won't be going anywhere today."

Standing up, Leslie experienced a sharp pain in her left temple, and suddenly the tree trunks and bushes began to sway. Her peripheral vision became gray and began closing in. Automatically her hand rose to her eyes, while her body swayed to adjust itself to her vision.

"Perfect. Now you're going to faint," the man said without a great deal of feeling.

Loath to give him the satisfaction of being what she knew he would consider a typical woman, Leslie swore, "I'd rather die," before unconsciousness overtook her.

Two

"So, what's it going to be? Are you going to die or what?" The deep, husky voice filtered through the darkness, reaching Leslie's consciousness, echoing painfully as it moved on into infinity.

Slowly she opened her eyes. Quickly she closed them again. She was totally blind. In that split second, she saw nothing but endless, empty darkness. Her throat constricted and tears of despair welled in her eyes. An irrepressible moan of misery escaped her as she moved her hand to pinpoint the source of the excruciating pain in her temple.

"If you're planning to die, don't. I've already wasted most of my day watching you sleep. I don't have time to dig you a grave, so I'm warning you, if you die, I'll leave you here for buzzard bait," came the male voice from seconds before.

Instinctively Leslie reopened her eyes. God was good. She could make out the bulky shadow of what appeared to be a very large man standing over her.

"Do you need my decision right away?" she muttered, closing her eyes again, grateful for the vision she had left and finding it less painful when she wasn't straining to see. "My head's killing me."

"I'm not surprised," the man stated matter-of-factly.

"It looks like you took a pretty good thump when you ran me off the road. Want me to light the lantern?"

Pain shot through Leslie's head and neck as she jerked them toward the man's voice and strove to focus her eyes once again.

"It's dark?" she asked bewilderedly. "It's nighttime?"

"Can't you see? Of course it's nighttime. It's pitch black out here," the man said, his voice gruff with anger—or concern, Leslie couldn't tell.

"Well, I thought I was going blind," she said a bit more testily than she meant to. But her memory was returning. The wedding, the impulsive trip into the mountains, the camper . . . she was beginning to feel more than a little discouraged.

Leslie heard an exasperated sigh and listened while the man moved toward her. There was a blinding flash of light as he struck a match. She followed the light and watched as the lantern came to life. Looking up, she saw a pair of clear, intense eyes holding hers so forcefully that a shiver passed through her and her skin began to prickle with fear . . . and excitement.

With those eyes, so shiny and deep, the man sought out Leslie's soul, the essence of her being. He asked silent questions and took the answers he wanted. Leslie had a peculiar feeling that he was reading her thoughts, absorbing her most intimate dreams and desires and was at the same time measuring and evaluating her character and values. She felt as if he were turning her inside out, and for some reason, she knew he was enjoying it.

He gave no outward sign of his pleasure, however. As he finished his assessment, he finally pronounced, "You're not blind. But you still have some explaining to do. Are you thirsty?" he asked absently, getting to his feet and walking off into the darkness.

As she watched his tall, lean frame move away, she had to admire the grace with which he moved. His shoulders were broad, and the plaid flannel shirt he wore couldn't conceal the large muscles that bulged beneath it. His legs were long and thick and powerful, but they moved with a loose fluidity that Leslie found oddly fascinating.

Suddenly her view was obscured by a huge blue mound that went straight up in the air like a dome. Leslie gasped as she realized it was the skirt of her dress and that everything under it was completely exposed. She tried to push it down but only succeeded in causing it to bounce around and increase her embarrassment at looking like a fool.

"Relax," the man said from somewhere beyond the cloud of pale blue silk and lace, "I can't see anything from my side either. Your petticoat covers up everything but your feet. Are they cold?" he asked as an afterthought. "I only had the one blanket, and I wasn't sure which end of you to cover."

Recalling the low cut of her bodice, Leslie was grateful for his decision and began to wonder if this awful day would ever come to an end.

"I don't have any aspirin with me," he said, not really apologizing as he moved back into the low circle of light. "But I was about to start a fire. At least you'll be a little warmer."

He came down on one knee and bent over Leslie. She experienced a sense of relief as she recalled that he wasn't as ominous looking up close as he was at a distance. Reluctantly she had to admit she liked his face. It wasn't conventionally handsome, but it was interesting in a rugged, earthy way.

He offered her water from a canning jar. When her neck wobbled under the strain of holding her head up, he slipped a hand to the back of her head to help her. Leslie was surprised at how warm and gentle his hand was. Nothing else about this man seemed warm or gentle.

"I hope you appreciate the restraint I'm using here in deference to your headache," he mentioned casually, his deep, thick voice devoid of humor. "It's not every day I have a beautiful woman in a fancy dress drive me off the road, call me a trespasser, and then faint dead away, you know."

Leslie tried to look surprised. "No?"

"No," he confirmed, pointedly. "And I want your story as soon as you can think straight. And it better be good."

The man put the water down beside the lantern, then turned his back to Leslie as he started the fire. She knew she owed him some sort of an explanation. Gruff and obviously put out as he was, he had taken care of her after she'd passed out. And she could feel that she was testing his patience sorely with every minute she remained silent. But how did one go about explaining to a stranger that one was an idiot.

Trying to find the best way of stating her case, Leslie found the events of the day as unbelievable as she was sure he would. Self-pity and spontaneous behavior were new to her. Leslie was normally calm, easygoing, and fairly certain there wasn't much in the world that was worth getting upset over. Everyone had problems, but to Leslie it had always been just a matter of choices. She'd floated through twenty-eight years of life being bright, capable, and financially sound. When conflicts arose, she had simply examined them, determined the direction she wanted to go with them, and solved them. Her life was simple and logical . . . most of the time. And she liked it that way . . . most of the time.

Her particular character traits were also the reason she enjoyed and performed her job so well. She liked facts and raw data. They didn't lie, they rarely changed, and there was nothing mysterious about them. They were simple and logical.

Those same traits, Leslie felt, were the sources of her greatest flaws. When something wasn't simple or logical to her, a compulsion to twist and mold them to be so overwhelmed her. Take love, for instance. Where was the simplicity and logic in that?

So how on earth was she going to explain all of this to a stranger? Would he understand that she was scared witless that she'd never be in love, because she didn't understand it, or that she'd never be loved, really loved, because it would wither and die waiting for her to recognize it? Should she tell him that she was terrified of discovering that the fondness she felt for Jeff Warner was actually love after all? That the friendly relationship they shared was as good as love got? That she was beginning to believe there were no such things as passion or deep abiding devotion or selfless giving and cherishing between two people?

On second thought, maybe she should just stick to the facts, she decided. He'd never believe she drove all the way up there to see something as powerful and moving as God's handiwork in the mountains just to prove to herself that she *was* capable of feeling something.

"I was supposed to be in a wedding this afternoon," she offered in a soft, tentative voice.

The man turned to look at her. He considered her for several long, tense moments before he arched a dark brow and asked, "Your own?"

"No. My sister's. I was supposed to be the maid of honor."

"I take it you didn't get to the church on time."

"Well, yes. I was there . . . but then I left."

"And came up here," he finished her story for her

in a dry tone of voice that normally would indicate it all made sense. They both knew it didn't.

Still, Leslie realized the man wouldn't care about all the events that had taken place between her arrival at the church and their accident on the mountain, so she said, "That's about it. Except that I haven't eaten all day. That may be another reason why I fainted. I've never fainted before, so it's hard to tell why I did today."

Again the man studied her face intently—and again Leslie felt like an open book. His eyes moved down her blue-silk-and-lace-clad body and back again. Finally he spoke. "You ever thought of writing short stories for a living?" he asked, his tone cynical but with the addition of his humor not biting. He smiled briefly, more to himself than at Leslie, and when she refused to comment, he said, "I suppose all the details are grossly personal and highly painful, and to recite them would have you in tears in seconds, so I won't ask for them right now. But for our survival, I need to know if someone's going to come looking for you when you don't show up tonight."

"I doubt it," Leslie said without hesitating. "Even if they called, they wouldn't think it out of the ordinary to get my answering machine, and tomorrow . . . well, I was supposed to be leaving town in the morning. I'm afraid it'll be at least two weeks before anyone misses me."

"Great." There was a long-suffering sigh. "I guess that settles that, then."

"What settles what?"

"I was hoping there'd be a husband or boyfriend waiting for you. Someone to start a search. In which case it would be easier for everyone if we stayed close to the cars so they'd find us faster. As it is, I guess I'll have to take you with me."

"Take me with you where?" Leslie asked, more than a little distracted.

"Home."

Leslie knew it would take several days to hike out of the mountains. Even if this charming fellow could find it in himself to loan her some more appropriate clothing, she was sure she couldn't endure the hardships of spending days on end alone with the man.

"I wouldn't want to put you out that way," Leslie said. "I could stay here. There's water at the creek, and I'm sure I could find some berries or something to eat. You'd make much better time without me. You could call my family and tell them exactly where they can come to get me. We wouldn't even have to bother with a rescue team."

"I don't have a phone," he said, watching her curiously. "And it's still a little early for berries."

"What about your neighbors or a gas station along the way or something. I could even give you the money for a pay phone," she said, grasping at straws, not worried about the berries.

"My nearest neighbor is twenty miles away and after that it's thirty more to the nearest ranger station. And frankly I don't have time to go visiting either one of them on foot."

"Where do you live?" she asked with a gasp as hopelessness and despair settled over her for the second time that day.

"A little more than ten miles that way," the man said, indicating with his dark head that he lived higher and deeper into the mountains.

"But—" Leslie stopped herself. She turned her head away from the man and looked straight out into the night as tears began to blur her vision.

"But what?" His question was more like a command for her to finish her sentence.

"I don't want to spend two weeks with you," she

admitted with her usual grace and tact, her voice quivering slightly for emphasis.

"Aw. Cheer up, beautiful. By the time they get around to searching this far into the mountains and find our cars, then track us down through my truck's registration papers, we could be looking at months here. But if it'll make you feel any better, I'm not real crazy about this myself."

"That's quite obvious, thank you."

"Good. I don't want us starting off on the wrong foot," he said in a deceptively affable voice.

He turned back to his fire, which had started to glow and snap noisily as it consumed the dry leaves and twigs. Depressed and feeling vulnerable, Leslie wanted to stand up to this pompous, obnoxious man. Never had anyone treated her so badly. He wasn't even pretending to be civil. And people thought *she* was unfeeling, she ruminated with an ironic half laugh. Well, she had plenty of feelings now, and not one of them was pleasant.

With great determination, she pushed herself into a sitting position and cried out in pain and alarm as her head began to throb, and at the same time, she felt the bodice of her dress fall away from her body. Quickly clutching the dress and the blanket over her bare breasts, she turned startled and accusing blue eyes on the man who was now facing her. He looked concerned until he saw the anger in her eyes, and then he frowned.

Before he could speak, Leslie attacked. "What have you done to me?"

"What?"

"I'm half naked," she stated, the implications of which were clearly audible in the tone of her voice.

The man actually laughed at her outrage. "When someone faints, you loosen their clothing. Even twelve-year-old Boy Scouts know that," he told her in a patronizing tone. "My intentions were honorable."

"Oh," Leslie uttered, somewhat mollified.

"But," he said quickly, moving back to her side, covering the short distance on his hands and knees so that when he stopped and looked at her, their eyes were level, mere inches apart, "I can't say I wasn't tempted to peek," he said, wickedly grinning and allowing his gaze to lower and take in all Leslie hadn't managed to cover with the blanket.

Her heart began to pound harder and faster. Her skin grew warm, and her muscles began to tremble.

"Stop that," she ordered him with great bravado, her chest heaving as she struggled to breathe.

"What?" he asked, his eyes round.

"Stop looking at me like that."

"Why? Do I make you nervous?" he asked, enjoying himself.

"A little," Leslie admitted, her eyes narrowed cautiously even while her chin tilted defiantly.

The strange man sat back on his haunches, resting his hands on his knees as he regarded Leslie with a great deal of humor sparkling in his eyes. Leslie, on the other hand, sat perfectly still, but she, too, was taking inventory with a leery eye.

His dark hair was wavy and thick, a little unruly, and he wore it longer than most of the men she knew. His skin was tanned golden, almost bronze, and there were little lines creased in his face that deepened when he smiled or thought something was amusing, as he obviously thought she was at the moment. Overall, Leslie had to admit, he was much better looking when he was happy as opposed to not so happy.

"Look, lady," he said finally, merriment still gurgling in his voice, "I can't even remember the last time I jumped an unconscious or unwilling woman.

But don't push me, because I'm not saying it hasn't entered the realm of possibilities here. I didn't give in to the temptation to peek while you were out, and even though I've found you provoking to an extreme since you ran me off the road, I haven't attacked you yet. So, if you watch your step, I think you can feel reasonably safe with me. Do you want me to zip up your dress for you?" he asked, his eyes daring her to test his control.

Swallowing hard, Leslie took up his challenge.

"Yes, please," she said, glad her voice sounded stronger than she felt.

Carefully, the man moved behind her. Leslie ground her teeth together and began to pray he wasn't a crazed maniac when she felt his big hands come to rest on her bare shoulders. She refused to release the scream that was building inside her when he slowly and purposefully glided his fingers enticingly down her back. Her mind ran amok when he slipped his fingers inside her dress.

"You'll have to stand up. I can't get the little thingie to move," he said with far less emotion than Leslie was feeling.

Performing the simple task of getting to her feet proved to be easier said than done. Hampered by the reams of material and the damnable hoop below the waist, she also had to contend with her aching head and precarious bodice. It was some time before a frustrated and exhausted Leslie gave up her efforts. She found her companion waiting patiently with his hands on his hips and an idiotic grin on his face.

"That's one hell of a dress you got there, lady. You must feel like you're living a nightmare from *Gone With the Wind*," he observed, shaking his head in wonder. "You want me to help you up?"

Something deep inside Leslie snapped. No longer was she the slightest bit grateful to this man, nor was she afraid of him. No longer did she care what he thought of her or if he was indeed a homicidal maniac. He had gone too far, and Leslie was spitting mad.

"Yes," she ground out through clenched teeth.

"Please," he reminded her good-naturedly.

"Yes, please," she said, seething.

He stretched a hand out across the ruffles and wiggled his fingers at her in a very irksome way. With no other option, Leslie had to take a firm grip on his hand and hope for the best.

This wasn't her day. His big hand covered hers almost entirely. It was calloused and strong; its grip warm and secure. In one firm tug, Leslie was vertical and moving forward until she came full force into the man's broad chest. Winded by the impact and overheated by her anger, Leslie stood stunned and breathless in the man's arms, her face only inches from his. She felt the need to pull away, but something inexplicable appeared in his eyes and kept her still.

The mocking humor in his expression of moments before was now laced with an undefined challenge, the indifference became almost a plea to take on his dare, and the scorn . . . the scorn had taken on a smoky cloud of mystery, it had become a puzzle for Leslie to solve, a question to answer.

The moment seemed to stretch out past forever, but in actuality, it was only a split second and was gone before Leslie was ready to release it. The idea that this man was in any way vulnerable appealed to her very much. But that feeling, too, was short lived when, in a flash, the man was full of arrogance and mischief once more.

"Then again, maybe I shouldn't have made such a hasty decision," he said as he lowered his head and boldly took Leslie's lips with his own.

At first Leslie was furious and tried to fight him off. But with her hands holding up the bodice of her dress, all she could do was squirm and try to pull away. When her movements only succeeded in allowing him to reestablish a firmer grip and give her a second kiss, Leslie decided to take a new approach. She stood perfectly still and the second his arms relaxed a little, she kicked him as hard as she could. It took her two attempts to finally hit his shin bone, but her reward was well worth her efforts.

He gasped in pain and immediately released her. When he did, she held her dress up with one hand and used the other to push him away. To Leslie's astonishment, as he held on to his leg he was also laughing uncontrollably.

"Don't you dare laugh at me," she shouted. "And don't you ever touch me like that again. Do you hear me?"

The man laughed harder at her indignation.

"I mean it! I'm sick of this." She stamped her foot once. "I'm sorry you're a nasty, ill-tempered, and extremely rude individual, but you're not going to take it out on me anymore. The accident wasn't all my fault. I refuse to take all the blame for it. And if I'm going to be such an imposition to you for the next two weeks—or so—well, I'd just as soon take my chances alone than put up with you."

By the time Leslie finished her tirade, the man had pulled himself together somewhat and stood watching her. His eyes held a certain humorous admiration, and his lips were still twitching at the corners, but at least he wasn't rolling on the ground in a convulsive fit of laughter.

"You're not very funny."

"No. You're right. I'm not," he said, his amused look having faded to a smirk and a twinkle. "If I promise to be a good boy from now on, will you let me zip up your dress?"

Leslie considered his offer with great misgivings. She was sure she shouldn't trust him, but she definitely wanted her dress zipped so she could have two free hands. Courageously and with all the dignity she could muster, Leslie turned her back to him.

Several endless seconds passed before she felt his presence behind her. All her senses were on red alert, on guard for the slightest untoward action. None came. With a minimum of movement, the man deftly secured her dress, said "There you go," and walked away.

But even though he'd amended his behavior, Leslie wasn't satisfied.

"Aren't you going to apologize?"

"For what?" The man didn't bother to look away from feeding the fire. He kept throwing twigs and small branches into the flames as if nothing out of the ordinary had happened between them.

"For being so rude and . . . and for what you did to me," Leslie said.

"I kissed you," he said, because she didn't seem able to identify the activity and he wanted to make his next point. "It wasn't exactly a rape. I could have used a little more finesse, I guess, but all in all, I'm not sorry I did it. So, I won't apologize."

"Honestly. You're the most insulting man I've ever met," Leslie said, disgusted.

"That's too bad. Maybe if you'd met a lowlife like myself sooner, you wouldn't be so snooty now," he said, turning to her at last.

"Snooty? Snooty? I am not snooty."

"Defensive, then."

"I'm only defensive when someone else is attacking. In this case, that's you."

The man seemed to be thinking her statement over. Leslie knew her argument was valid and drew confidence from it. The man finally nodded twice and said, "Maybe in the beginning, when I was still in shock. But I took care of you when you passed out, and that was nice of me. And since you woke up, I think I've been pretty civil."

"You kissed me," she said in an accusing tone.

"Oh. Well, that was bound to happen eventually anyway. I just figured that as long as we were in the right position, we might as well get it over with."

"What?" Leslie's face was a grimace of shocked disbelief. Was this man not only rude and vulgar, but insane as well, she wondered.

"Let's face it, I'm reasonably good-looking. You've got all the right parts, very nicely put in all the right places. We're alone in the woods together and most likely will be for some time to come. We were bound to kiss eventually," he said, in a very matter-of-fact way.

"What?" she repeated, more and more convinced that she was stranded in the mountains with a madman.

"Come on, . . . What is your name?"

"Leslie."

"Leslie, what?"

"Rothe. What's yours?" she asked, not really sure she wanted to know, fairly certain by now that it could be found on the F.B.I.'s ten-most-wanted list.

"Joe Bonner," he said. "And I think that human nature being what it is, we each would have started wondering what it would be like to kiss the other sooner or later anyway. I just wondered sooner, is all. There's no need to make a federal case out of a simple little kiss, Leslie."

"There is if you won't apologize for it," Leslie said doggedly.

"I'm not sorry. I admit I might have enjoyed it more if you'd cooperated a little, but it wasn't so bad as it was."

Leslie gasped in frustration and anger. There was no dealing with him. He was impossible to talk to, she decided, as she pulled the blanket tighter around her shoulders and began to walk away from him.

"If you're going off to visit the bushes, you should stay on the road and out of the underbrush. You'd probably hang yourself in that dress. Go up around the bend if you want," he said in an annoyingly omniscient way.

Leslie glared at him over her shoulder but took his advice nonetheless. Making her way clumsily through the darkness in her high-heeled shoes, her mind automatically switched to her problem-solving mode. In her usual way, she quickly identified her problems: The man, Joe Bonner, and being stranded in the mountains with him. Objectives: Get rid of this Joe Bonner person and get home safely. Solutions: The answer to the first problem was easy. Shoot Joe Bonner at the first opportunity. The second problem was not as easily solved. And, unfortunately, it looked as if she was going to need Joe Bonner to accomplish it.

On her way back to the fire—and Joe Bonner—a calmer Leslie decided she simply would have to grit her teeth and bear with the impossible man until she was rescued or until she could come up with another answer to her dilemma.

In the meantime, she knew of another problem she could easily solve. Knowing there was little of her to see under the skirt of her gown because of the additional slips she'd worn, she freely gathered up the silk and lace in one hand and began untying the strings of the hooped skirt with the other. With the hoops gone, the dress hung straight to the ground. It was now far too long but much less cumbersome.

Well satisfied, Leslie looked up to find the man—as she preferred to think of him—watching her. Something in the way he was regarding her made her feel agitated and uneasy. He nodded his approval of what she had done and said, "Good idea."

"Thank you so much," she said stiffly.

"Definitely snooty," he said as if it was a final judgment of her character.

Leslie walked over to the man and strangled him with her bare hands—but only in the back of her mind, where she kept her fondest wishes and desires. In reality she gathered her skirts once again, ignoring the man, and settled herself on the tarpaulin where she'd been lying before. With great flair, she arranged the silk and lace over her legs and drew the blanket closer around her bare shoulders.

"You hungry?" he asked.

"Yes," she said. Cannibalism flashed through her mind as a possible solution to one of her problems. But she quickly discarded the idea, assuming it would be rather tasteless, both literally and figuratively.

Two pieces of bread landed in her lap. The slices were stuck firmly together, but with the aid of the light from the fire, Leslie could see the adhesive was either an appetizing pâté or peanut butter. Considering the sandwich's origins, she assumed it was peanut butter. However, she wasn't altogether disappointed or ungrateful. She was very hungry.

"Where did this come from?" she asked between bites, not caring that the food stuck to the roof of her mouth.

"I was on my way back from getting groceries when we met on the road," he said, choosing his words carefully. "My truck is full of food."

"And now it'll all go to waste." She shook her head regretfully.

"Hardly. We'll take as much as we can carry in the morning. And I'll make another trip down for the nonperishables in a couple of days."

Leslie nodded. This made sense to her, and she'd always believed in carrying her share of the load. Basically a city person and not overly fond of outdoor sports, she really wasn't looking forward to the hike through the mountains. But she vowed she'd accomplish it with as much grace as possible. She'd show him snooty.

They were silent through most of the meal. Leslie took a second helping, her host went back for thirds. He'd boiled coffee in a saucepan and asked, or rather told her to hold a filter over two pint-size canning jars while he poured the hot, dark fluid into each.

"I wasn't planning on a camp out," he said, needlessly explaining his lack of equipment.

Leslie had to admire his ingenuity. The coffee was strong and hot, warming her from the inside out, which was more than she could say for either the fire or her blanket. While the heat of the fire did a fair job of warding off the cold night air in front of her, the chilling breeze seemed to catch and settle in the blanket that lay around her shoulders and across her back.

After her third rather obvious shiver, Joe got to his feet and came over to her side of the fire.

"Scoot up," he told her.

"What for?" she asked, confused and suspicious at once.

"I'll sit behind you and keep the wind off your back."

"That's not necessary. I'm perfectly—"

"Perfect. I know," he broke in on her objection. "But if we're going to survive this night without the right gear, we're going to have to keep each other warm. My jacket will hold off the wind. So we'll sit on the tarp facing the fire with me at your back."

No longer confused, Leslie focused her attention on her distrust of this man. "If you think I'm going to give you a second chance to manhandle me, you're crazy," she said, pulling the blanket closer, glaring up at him stubbornly.

Again, he mocked her with laughter.

"You're certainly full of yourself, aren't you? I give you one little kiss and suddenly you're irresistible to me? Is that what you think?"

"No," she said. "What I think is that you're a lunatic or maybe an axe murderer. The nicest thing I've thought so far was that you're just some poor thing who wandered out the front gates of an asylum and can't quite get the hang of being normal."

"Hey. You're all heart, aren't you? I'll have to be careful not to let your high opinion of me swell my head," he said. He didn't appear to be offended at all, but he certainly was wearing a peculiar expression. At first Leslie thought he was still amused, but for a fleeting second there was almost a look of admiration in his eyes, and then it was gone, replaced by the thoughtful, considering look she was growing very familiar with. "However, flattered as I am, I am none of those things. I am hard to live with sometimes, which is why I spend a lot of time alone up here in my cabin. But you don't need to be afraid of me. I am both safe and sane, and I won't hurt you." He paused briefly. "I won't even touch you again without your permission. How's that?"

"That's how it should have been from the beginning," Leslie pointed out, still wary.

"True. But be that as it may, I think I can prove to you how harmless I really am and that I'm not such a bad guy after all, if you'll allow me to."

Leslie was doubtful, but for some inane reason she wanted to believe him. A lot of it had to do with his being the only other human for miles around, and some of it had to do with Leslie's basic good nature. But that still left a small part of the reason unaccounted for, a part that made Leslie feel uncomfortable and excited at the same time, a part she didn't want to examine too closely just yet.

Leslie gave her nonverbal consent for the experiment to begin. This time she was sure of the approval she saw in his eyes, and even though he didn't actually smile, he did look pleased.

Three

"Now I know you're nuts," Leslie told Joe several minutes later. "There's no way I'm going to crawl in there with you."

He had placed the tarpaulin lengthwise beside the fire. She'd watched as he stretched his long body out across the far half and covered himself with half the blanket. Panic had overtaken her quickly when he held up the other half of the blanket invitingly and motioned for her to get in beside him.

"Then you'll freeze to death," he pointed out casually. "And I won't get a chance to prove what a perfect gentleman I can be when I set my mind to it."

Leslie gave a very unladylike snort, and said, "You blew your chance at that hours ago."

When the "experiment" began, she had stood up when he asked her to. Now she shivered as the frigid wind blew, chilling her to the bone.

"I want my blanket back," she said, her voice sounding very childlike, even to herself.

"It's my blanket and we'll share it," Joe said. "And hurry it up, my arm is getting tired."

Leslie frowned in displeasure for several more seconds, and then, as she was once again caught in an icy breeze, she said, "You're an easy person not to like, Mr. Bonner."

She could feel him watching her as she lay down beside him facing the fire. She welcomed the shelter of the blanket as he covered her with it. She wouldn't admit it out loud, but between the blanket, the fire, and the man, she could feel the warmth almost immediately. It felt like a blessing.

"Comfy?" Joe asked.

"Hardly."

"Warm at least?"

"Barely."

"Want my coat? You, the blanket, and my thermals ought to keep me warm through the night. That dress of yours and just the blanket aren't much protection."

"I'll be fine," Leslie said in a tone that left no room for argument. She was convinced her anger would keep her warm.

"Do you want to tell ghost stories, or should we just go to sleep?" he asked, a teasing quality creeping into his voice.

"You may do as you please, Mr. Bonner," she said, "I'm going to sleep to escape this horrible dream."

"You can call me Joe, if you want."

"I don't *want* to call you anything. I want to go to sleep," she said, knowing it wasn't likely to happen with him literally breathing down her neck. His breath was warm against her cool skin and made goose bumps break out across her back.

"Well, before you do, could you tell me where I can put this hand?" he asked, holding his free arm out above her. "I don't want to get you all stirred up again by putting it somewhere you don't want it to be."

"How considerate, Mr. Bonner," she said acidly, trying to shut out thoughts of the first place that had come to mind. Taking his arm, she laid it firmly along his own hip and leg. "How's that?"

"Stiff and awkward. But for you . . . I'll try it."

Leslie made another small, disdainful noise in her throat and wiggled into a more comfortable position, getting as close to his body as she could without actually touching him. Gradually her muscles began to relax, and her bones seemed to thaw. And when Joe made no further attempt to talk to her or touch her, she allowed herself to become lulled into a semiconscious state of tranquillity.

"So, what happened at this wedding you arrived at but didn't get to?" Joe asked, after a long while, sounding as drowsy as she felt.

Leslie tried to put her defense shields back in place, but she was too tired. It had been an extremely long and exhausting day filled with one personal revelation after another, and they weighed heavily on her heart. It occurred to her that talking about it might make her feel better . . . but to Joe Bonner? She'd heard of people talking to plants and other inanimate objects as a form of therapy. This man, who in her opinion had no heart and didn't give a whit of concern about the way she felt, would be as good as any tree to talk to, she supposed.

"My sister locked herself in the bathroom," Leslie finally answered.

Joe made a funny little noise in the back of his throat. "Why?" he asked.

Leslie sighed. She wasn't sure if she wanted to go to all the trouble of explaining it to him. "It's a long story."

"Well, I'm not exactly comfortable, so I'll probably be awake all night anyway," Joe said, using his own unique form of encouragement.

Leslie's eyes were closed, and she left them that way as she tried to decide where to start.

"It was my fault. I—"

"If you slept with her boyfriend, I don't want to hear this," Joe said.

"Oh!" she gasped. "Really. You are the most disgusting man." She pulled the blanket closer around her shoulders as if to form a stronger barrier between them. "I'd never dream of doing such a thing, not to mention that he's not at all my type."

"So what's your type?"

"I . . . well, I have . . . I want," Leslie stammered. Her mind was a blank. Jeff Warner's face flashed briefly in her mind but was gone quickly. She knew in that instant Jeff was not the man she was looking for. But if not Jeff, then who? "I'm not sure what my type is," she said, angry at having to admit it.

Joe was silent for several seconds. Then he quite nonchalantly asked, "Are you gay?"

It wasn't easy but Leslie managed to roll over onto her stomach. She turned her face to meet Joe's, and glared at him haughtily.

He had the grace to look startled by her reaction. "Well, I was only asking. There aren't many women your age who have no idea of what they're looking for in a man. Haven't you ever been in love?"

Put on the defensive once again, Leslie couldn't maintain her angry stare. Looking back at the fire, she gave into another impulse, the second one that day. This time it was to lie. "Of course I have," she muttered in a low voice.

"No, you haven't," Joe said, coming up on one elbow, delighted with his discovery. "I'll bet you can't even tell me what you *don't* want in a man."

"I know I don't want anyone like you."

"Of course. What else?"

Leslie paused to consider the question. Then slowly she said, "I don't want someone like me either."

"Explain."

"I've been too involved with myself, my career, and the material things I want out of life to pay much attention to what's going on around me. I've . . . lost touch with the things that are really important in life."

"Like?"

Leslie looked at Joe. His expression was one of interest. There was no mischief or mockery in his eyes, just mild curiosity.

"Like nature," she said, using her hands to indicate the land she'd built a career on by betraying it. "Like people and how and why they feel as they do sometimes. There's a lot about human nature that, well, that I just don't understand."

"Like what?" he asked.

"Oh . . . ," Leslie pretended to be thoughtfully picking a subject, but there was only one uppermost in her mind at the moment. "Love, for instance. How do people know when they're in love?"

Too late she realized she had admitted to his accusation of never having been in love, but he didn't seem to be inclined to press the point. Instead his green eyes were intense and very serious.

"They don't know when they're in love. They feel it," he said, answering her question sincerely as if she were a child. "It's an emotion. You don't always have a reason for feeling the way you do, do you?"

Leslie pondered this. "As a matter of fact, I do."

Joe frowned, then asked, "What's your favorite color?"

"Red."

"Why?"

"It's a bright, warm color, and I look good in it."

Joe's frown deepened. "Do you ever get what they call the 'blues?' "

"On the twenty-fourth or twenty-fifth day of my cycle I'll sometimes be a little out of sorts."

"I suppose you always know exactly why you're happy or sad or angry or jealous of someone too," he said, beginning to get a picture of Leslie's problem.

"Of course. Why would I feel those things if I didn't?"

"Well, you took an instant dislike to me, and you didn't even know me," he pointed out.

"I don't need to. I know exactly why I don't like you," she said, then went on to list her reasons. "You're rude, you're presumptuous, you like to be threatening sometimes, you're crude, conceited, and you're grumpy."

"But other than that I'm okay, right?"

Leslie slid him a sidelong glance. "That remains to be seen," she said, and then she smiled.

Maybe he's a little better than a tree, she thought, feeling almost happy for the first time in quite a while. At least this distempered man made her feel things. Shock, outrage, and distrust were preferable to a constant diet of apathy.

A slow grin spread across Joe's face before he said, "You're something else, lady. I'm not too sure what you are yet, but you're definitely something else. Tell me, does any of this have anything to do with your sister locking herself in the bathroom?"

Leslie nodded. She folded her arms and pillowed her head with them. Briefly she hit on the highlights of her morning, culminating with, "My parents all but asked me to leave. I don't even know if my sister's married right now or not."

She felt Joe's hand move under the blanket and over her bare back. It moved slowly up to her neck, where he began a gentle massage. Leslie's first impulse was to pull away, but his touch was so warm and the careful kneading of her neck muscles was so relaxing, she was hard put to move at all.

Blissfully she allowed her eyes to close. From far away she heard the man speak. "I have to admit, it doesn't sound as if you've had the best of days. But none of this explains why you're up here in the mountains."

" 'Nother long story," Leslie mumbled.

"And why do I get the feeling I won't be hearing it tonight?" Joe asked, receiving no answer.

Joe Bonner didn't remove his hand from Leslie's back nor did he sleep. Long after her breathing had become deep and regular, Joe's hand continued to glide lightly over her warm, soft skin. He enjoyed the feel of it, and he liked the way she looked when she was sleeping. He liked the way she looked when she was awake, too, but he was sure she wouldn't allow him to stare at her as he was now.

He couldn't help wondering about her. She was like an angel from out of nowhere—suddenly there, breathtakingly beautiful, and full of spirit. She'd knocked him for a loop the first time he'd really looked at her. From that point on, she had only become more and more intriguing to him.

It amazed him that no one had staked their claim to her yet. That no man had taught her to love floored him. The inclination to teach her himself was very strong, but a woman like Leslie Rothe was the last thing he wanted or needed in his life.

The evil temptation to reveal the secrets of love to her, to possess her body and soul and then break her heart crept into his mind, but he quickly banished it. It was natural and very human to want to hurt someone as badly as he had been hurt, but he knew he shouldn't and wouldn't act on the desire. Especially with this woman, who obviously would have no idea what was happening to her. She had probably broken a hundred hearts just being so incredibly naive. Men had probably been throwing themselves at her feet for years, but for some reason, she'd never noticed it.

How many women had specific reasons attached to everything they felt? Better yet, he thought, how many refused to feel something because they had no reason to? Had he ever met a woman who didn't use "just because" as a reason or an excuse to react to any given situation? Joe didn't think so.

Idly he traced the shape of her body from shoulder to hip with his hand. It would be interesting to pit her against the other women he'd known, he thought. Would her overabundance of logic be an asset or a detriment? Would lying and cheating be on her list of acceptable ways to get what she wanted? Or would this woman be as honest as she was rational in achieving her goals?

Joe was trying to visualize a trustworthy woman with a syllogistic mind, when Leslie began to stir in her sleep. She turned toward him and burrowed closer, seeking his warmth. Joe frowned and shied away. Resting beside her was one thing, having her pressed up against him was quite another. It didn't matter that he was totally dressed and wearing a down parka besides. Just knowing that with the flick of a zipper she'd be completely exposed to him from the waist up was like lighting a string of firecrackers under his libido.

He tried to ease himself away without waking her, but she only renewed her unconscious efforts. He was giving some serious thought to leaving their makeshift bed altogether, when she groaned and began to shiver. Joe grimaced even as his arms folded about her, automatically pulling her close to him, trying to warm her. He slid his hand between them and unzipped his jacket. Instinctively Leslie was drawn to the greater heat of his body. She wrapped her arms about him securely, while Joe enfolded her in his coat, trying to share as much of it as he could with her.

Leslie wiggled into a comfortable position, tucking her head neatly under Joe's chin. He heard her soft moan of satisfaction and rolled his eyes heavenward. The woman was enough to try the patience of a saint, he decided. And everyone who knew him knew he was no saint. Her hair smelled sweet and clean, and holding her was too easy; she fit in his arms too well.

Was he supposed to sleep like this, he wondered skeptically. His mind dared him to try, while his body made its own intentions perfectly clear. There would be no sleep for Joe Bonner tonight, was the message he got.

Joe sighed heavily in resignation. "Women," he said very like a curse. Then he closed his eyes and fought for control as Leslie stirred in his arms once more.

Leslie was toasty warm, but the right side of her body was sore and aching. She tried to readjust her position, but it did little good. Her eyes, heavy with sleep, opened slowly.

The world was cloaked in grayness. Just looking at it made Leslie cold. A gelid wind brushed across her left cheek, and she blindly buried her face deeper into the soft warmth at her right. Thick, hard bonds tightened about her possessively, and a peculiar sensation rippled through her body in response.

Leslie's eyes opened wide, and this time she was alert to her surroundings. Her nose was pressed tightly against red plaid flannel, and out of the corner of her eye all she could see was army green.

She quickly came up on one elbow and peered

down at Joe Bonner. He opened one eye, then closed it again, saying, "Now what?"

Embarrassed beyond belief, Leslie stammered and said, "I . . . nothing . . . I'm sorry. I must have gotten cold in the middle of the night . . . or something."

"Must have," he agreed, yawning rudely in her face. "And it still is the middle of the night, so go back to sleep."

"No. No, I think the sun is beginning to rise," she said, observing the dull gray lightness around them. She noted, for the first time, that their campsite was smack in the middle of the road, very near the place where they almost had collided.

"Dawn in my book is still the middle of the night," he said drowsily. "Go to sleep."

"Well, actually, most people hold to the general consensus that the day begins at dawn, although technically it begins at midnight. But I think the idea is that if it's light out, it's day," Leslie said, realizing how foolish she sounded but unable to stop the nervous prattle that was falling from her lips.

Accustomed to coming awake slowly, it was a jolt to Leslie's system to wake up and instantly have to feel awkward and agitated. Recalling their final discussion of the night before only increased her mortification. Where had the idea that this man could pass as a tree come from, she wondered.

Slowly Joe turned his head to look at her. She couldn't tell if he was angry, amused, or thinking about throwing a net over her. After several seconds, in a voice that was quiet and most sincere, he said, "The next two weeks are going to be very long, aren't they?"

Leslie didn't know how to respond, and she no longer could hold his incredulous gaze. She began to slide away from him, carefully, so as not to disturb him anymore than was necessary.

"I'll be very quiet if you want to go back to sleep," she said, growing cold again as his hands slipped away from her. "I'll gather wood or something for the fire. I want to do my share. In fact, I think we should keep track of the food I eat, and then once I get home, I'll mail you a check to reimburse you."

Joe made no reply. He continued to stare at her as if she'd suddenly turned green and grown antennae.

"Are you okay?" Leslie asked, concerned. It hadn't as yet been confirmed that he wasn't some sort of escapee, although he had proved to be trustworthy during the night. Perhaps it was simply time for his medication, she thought sympathetically.

He sat up suddenly and without answering her question, removed his coat and tossed it to her. "Put this on," he ordered.

"Oh, no. I can use—"

"Look, lady," he said, breaking in on Leslie's objection in his usual discourteous way, "I don't plan to argue with you everytime I say something. Just leave me alone and do what I say and we'll get along fine."

Shocked by his sudden outburst, Leslie watched as Joe got to his feet. He looked as though he was as stiff and sore as she was, and it made her heart glad. As to how to react to his disposition, she wasn't sure. If she were a man, she'd punch him in the nose. But his superior strength was too obvious for her to entertain that notion for long. And she certainly didn't want to push him over the edge if he was, indeed, mentally unstable. Her best course of action, she decided, was to try to get along with him.

Wordlessly she sat up and put the man's coat on.

It retained some of his body heat and felt wonderful, but she was certain he didn't want to hear about it.

She saw him nod his satisfaction and watched as he picked up the pan and canning jars they'd used the night before, then stomped off into the woods, taking the blanket with him.

Leslie sighed her disappointment. Aside from his rather queer personality, Joe Bonner was a very physically appealing man. His long, thick legs and broad, muscled shoulders held a certain fascination for her and initiated the oddest sensation deep in her abdomen. And she found she was growing quite used to his "un" appearance. Leslie laughed softly. It was a good description for Mr. Bonner. He was untailored, unclipped, unshaven, and . . . unusual to her.

Joe Bonner was an odd man indeed, Leslie decided as she got to her feet and began stretching her aching muscles. The previous night he'd seemed genuinely interested in her plight. The best part of him, his eyes, had shown his concern. They'd shown his wonder and surprise. She'd seen warmth and understanding in their depths and that had made it easier for her to talk to him. This morning, he appeared distant, guarded, and hostile again.

"And they say women have severe mood swings," Leslie muttered ironically.

"As long as we're up, we might as well get started," Joe said, making his announcement a short while later as he strode back into their campsite. He obviously had been to his truck, as the blanket he now carried over one shoulder was tied like a knapsack and filled to the point of bulging.

"What about breakfast?" Leslie asked, not as hungry as she was reluctant to start hiking.

"I don't eat breakfast," he said.

"Well, I do."

Joe considered this for several seconds, then said, "There's dry cereal and milk or another peanut butter sandwich. Do you need coffee too?"

"If it's no bother."

"It's a hell of a lot of bother, but if it'll keep you from whining all the way up the mountain, we'll make some."

"I don't whine," Leslie said, not really arguing, just stating a fact.

"Are you used to hiking?"

"No, but I jog at my health club, and I'm strong," she said in self-defense. "Besides, I'm just not the whiny type."

"There's that 'type thing' again," he said. "I suppose you have everyone you meet tucked into nice, neat little stereotypes, huh?"

"No, not exactly. I think there are certain basic types of people, but I also believe people are very different from one another," Leslie said. She wanted to tell him that she'd started a whole new category just for him but thought better of it.

Joe tilted his head to one side, a slow sly grin spreading out across his face. "In that case, I'll make you a little wager."

"What?"

"I'll bet you another long, juicy kiss—with cooperation this time—that before the day is over, you'll find something to whine about."

Leslie swallowed hard. "What do I get when you lose?"

"Anything you want," he said confidently—too confidently.

"You're on."

"What are you planning to do with all of that?" he asked, changing the subject rather quickly as he indicated the large pile of firewood Leslie had gathered during his absence. "Build a rescue fire?"

"No. It's for the fire. I was trying to be helpful," Leslie said, keeping her voice low and humble on purpose, trying to shame him for his ingratitude.

Joe cast Leslie a calculating glance, and right away she knew she hadn't fooled him. "Cereal or sandwich?" he asked in a very dry tone of voice.

"Sandwich, I guess." She wanted something that would stick to her ribs.

"Good."

"Why good?" she asked, curious.

"Well, I forgot to take a spoon with me when I went shopping yesterday. I was having visions of your having to eat with your fingers and my having to hear about it all day."

Leslie was getting very tired of his verbal abuse and wasn't sure how much more of it she was going to take. But for the moment, she was determined to get along with him. Keeping her mouth firmly closed, she made and ate her breakfast while Joe made coffee.

There was silence throughout the meal. Leslie was beginning to think she could learn to enjoy the whispering of the wind through the trees and the occasional birdcall. They weren't the city noises she was more familiar with, but they had a sort of intimate and reassuring quality of their own.

Leslie looked up to find her companion holding a very lethal looking knife. It was eight to ten inches long and two inches wide. It glimmered in the sunlight. She could feel all the blood draining from her face; her heart stopped, then kicked into a wild, erratic rhythm. The man *was* a maniac. Of all the times in her life to be right in her thinking, she wished this hadn't been one of them.

"Oh, no." She gasped in horror as Joe stood and advanced toward her. "Please don't."

"It has to be done," he said calmly, his attitude determined.

"No. No, it doesn't. We can work something out," Leslie said, her voice pleading. She would have given anything to see her parents just one more time.

"I can't see any other way around this. If you don't make a big fuss about it, it'll be a lot easier for both of us."

"A big fuss?" she repeated in amazement, staring up at him as he stood before her, his gaze firm and calculating. Was she supposed to sit placidly and let him kill her, she wondered in a daze.

Coming to her senses, Leslie bolted away from him. But he was as quick as he was strong. He grabbed at the silk and lace of her skirt and held on, impeding her escape. Leslie took a hard fall to the ground but immediately turned to face him. Tears welled in her eyes as a very strange expression formed on his face.

"Dammit, I'm trying to help you. It's only a dress. You can buy yourself ten more just like it when you get home, but you'll never make it up that mountain unless we cut it off," Joe said, amazed and very put off by her reaction.

"Oh," she said, her voice cracking as her emotions drained away leaving her feeling weak and very much like a fool. "Yes. I see what you mean."

Joe frowned, his eyes wary as he watched her for several seconds. Then leaving her on the ground, he gathered up a length of material and began to cut off nearly two feet of it all the way around.

"Do you want to save the slip or do you want me to cut it too?" Joe asked Leslie, who had been watching him silently with a dull expression on her face.

"I . . . I'll take it off."

"Are you sure? The more layers you have on, the warmer you'll be, you know," he told her, extending a hand to help her up when she made no effort to help herself.

Leslie came to a sitting position on her own, and holding her hand out, she said, "I'll cut it off myself, then, if you'll loan me your knife."

Taking a careful assessment of her emotional state, Joe finally handed the knife to her, handle first. Leslie could hardly look him in the eye. If she had no emotions as some people claimed, how could she have acted so stupidly, she wondered. Joe Bonner was probably thinking she was as mentally unstable as she had thought he was.

Joe walked back down to his truck while Leslie finished redesigning her clothing. Just as she finished, he returned carrying a large cooler. She stood idly by, not knowing what to do to help, while he divided his perishable groceries between the blanket and the tarpaulin. The blanket contained the least of the supplies. He laced a short length of rope through the holes in the tarp and then gathered them like purse strings. He then tied two of the corners of the blanket together and stopped.

He appeared to be having a serious mental debate as he sat very still, his hands clasped loosely between his knees. Eventually he looked up at Leslie and said, "You have another major decision to make. I want you to try and remain calm, okay?"

A sense of foreboding washed through Leslie. "I'll try," she said bravely in a small voice, even though the fact that he was treating her like a brainless idiot rankled her.

Joe held up a pair of worn sneakers that Leslie hadn't noticed had been lying on the ground beside him. "I found these in the truck. If they'll stay on your feet, you can wear them, or I can break the heels off your shoes."

Leslie looked from his shoes to hers and then

back again. The relief she felt was short-lived as her temper began to boil.

"Even if I get the heels off those, they'll be uncomfortable and hard to walk in. And although these aren't very fashionable, I thought you might not get as bent out of shape if we could save your shoes," he said.

Feeling extremely indignant and infuriated, and well aware of what he must be thinking of her, Leslie smiled stiffly and said, "Thank you. It was very thoughtful of you."

Joe shrugged off her gratitude and tossed her the shoes. "I brought your purse up from your car. There wasn't much else there. Do you want it, or should I put it in your pack?"

"My pack, please," she told him, as she finished tying the second sneaker. They were several sizes too big, but laced tightly, they did stay on her feet. "Will we be dressing for dinner at your cabin?"

Joe turned to face her. "Hardly," he said, not even trying to hide the sarcasm in his voice.

"Good," she said cheerfully. "Then I won't be needing these." As a gesture to show him she wasn't as vain and impractical as he had misjudged her to be, Leslie threw her high-heeled shoes far into the bushes. She was very proud of herself when she turned back to Joe.

Instead of approval, however, she saw that Joe was even more confused and wary of her than before.

"I don't care about the shoes or the dress," she said with feeling. "I behaved badly before, but it wasn't because of the dress. I didn't know what you were planning to do with that knife."

Joe searched her face long and hard, then he laughed. "Lady, you take the cake," he said. "If I was going to kill you, why didn't I do it last night?"

It was Leslie's expression more than her silence

that told him she had no idea as to what motivated an unstable personality, let alone what motivated Joe Bonner. "Okay," he said, "I admit I don't always act and sound as reasonable as I should, and you'll soon discover I am very hard to live with, like I told you before, but I can assure you that I'm as rational as . . . ," he paused, "Well, I'm *not* a lunatic. You're perfectly safe with me."

Even with his assurances that no harm would come to her, Leslie still had her doubts about her safety. It was the second time she'd seen him with a genuine smile on his face and heard him laugh in a way that wasn't meant to be a form of mental torture. Her skin prickled and little chills of excitement raced up and down her spine.

His merriment and then his smile faded away as they stood several feet apart reevaluating one another. Long, intense moments passed by before Joe finally broke the silence. He cleared his throat loudly and said in a thick, strained voice, "We'd better go."

He bent to gather up the two untied ends of the blanket and began to tie the supplies to Leslie's back. "We'll carry the cooler between us, but if it gets too heavy, let me know," he said.

"I'll manage," she said.

Joe stood back to examine his morning's work. He took in Leslie's rumpled mass of dark hair, her eyes, and the bruise on her left temple. Then his gaze moved lower to his too big and bulky down jacket and to the ragged-edged, pale blue silk and lace that hung below it. And there was no missing the bruises and scratches on her legs—or the huge clownlike shoes.

"Lord. You look horrible," he said, chuckling.

Leslie didn't have to look to know he was speaking the truth. She could well imagine how awful and ridiculous she looked. "This is what I've come to in less than a day at your hands," she said.

"No wonder you don't trust me." Joe picked up his tarpaulin knapsack and threw it over his shoulder. He took one handle of the cooler and waited for Leslie to take the other. With a teasing grin, he said, "Come on, Bozo. Let's stop clowning around and get this show on the road."

Leslie groaned at his play on words, but she lumbered faithfully alongside him as he led her deeper into the heart of the Colorado Rockies, her shoes flopping rhythmically as she went.

Four

"I . . . don't . . . whine. I . . . don't . . . whine," Leslie repeated to herself in time with each grueling step she took.

Hours that seemed more like weeks had passed, and not once had this extremely irritating man, Joe Bonner, offered to stop so she could rest.

The first couple of miles hadn't been too bad. Still well below the timberline, the terrain was rough and rocky and would have been much harder to traverse if not for the old logging road. She found the mountains breathtakingly beautiful, with every gap in the dense virgin forest revealing a new and unique glimpse of their splendor. Above them loomed snow-capped peaks and jagged rock formations that looked extremely treacherous for all their magnificence. She took comfort in knowing she didn't have to go anywhere near them.

She'd had a lot to think about in the first few hours. Picking up where she'd left off the day before, she still couldn't justify in her heart the destruction of the mountain for the sake of progress. It wasn't even for progress, she decided despondently. It was for the entertainment of those who could afford it. For fun.

Her stomach grew tight and began to burn at the thought that once violated, the slopes and valleys before her, never before touched except by the hands of God and a few lumberjacks, would fall prey to countless more abuses. It made her sick to think that simply because the numbers added up correctly and the facts supported the theory and she had been foolishly ambitious, a chain of ecological changes had been set into motion that could never be reversed. Once destroyed, this land could never be duplicated.

For a while it was hard for her to remember how much her Chinese art collection meant to her or why she had bought into a co-op instead of renting an apartment. Had the money, the recognition, and the prestige from a job well done been worth it?

She couldn't bring herself to answer. Instead she'd come to a standstill and put down her end of the cooler. Wordlessly, without giving her companion the slightest bit of attention, she removed the down jacket and tied the sleeves around her waist. The cool mountain air felt glorious as it fluttered across her bare shoulders and upper chest, which had grown flushed and overheated in her efforts to keep up with Joe's unmercifully long strides.

When she bent to pick up the cooler and resume the trek, she found that Joe had unburdened himself as well. She watched as he removed his flannel shirt. She sucked in a deep breath and felt a rush of heat pass through her as he stood before her in a bright white T-shirt pulled taut over flesh and muscle that bulged beneath it and anchored into jeans that hung low on his narrow hips. When he held the flannel shirt out to her, she just stared at him, her heart racing uncontrollably.

"Here," he said, indicating she was to put it on.

"Oh. Thanks, but I'm fine. The cool breeze feels great," she said on a shuddering breath.

"Put it on. The weather up here is deceptive. The sun'll fry you like bacon, and you won't even feel it until tonight. And," he added, his eyes lowering and lingering on the soft upper slopes of her breasts, "you don't want to ruin all that beautiful white skin of yours."

As if on cue, her chest rose and fell under his gaze as she automatically drew in a deep gulp of air. His insolence was wearing on her nerves, but she knew he was telling the truth about the sun—not because she knew it to be true, but because she was beginning to understand him. He wouldn't have gone to the trouble of removing his shirt for her if he didn't have a good reason. And she'd have bet her new pasta maker that his reason wasn't concern for her. He was ensuring himself against a night of having to listen to her whine about her sunburn—as if she would.

With the shirt on Leslie's back and the cooler in tow, they continued their hike. They didn't speak and rarely looked at each other directly, but they were both aware of the other, of being alone together in the forest.

Ignoring her peripheral vision and keeping her eyes trained straight ahead, Leslie focused her mind on a few of her other problems at hand: Her job, or rather what she'd done as part of her job for one.

She disliked being called a yuppie, but she had to admit she did fit the bill. She liked to work and enjoyed the power and money that it brought her. She couldn't bring herself to feel shame for her whole career. She worked hard and took great pains to make sure her efforts were as flawless as possible. When Leslie Rothe made a recommendation in a room full of wealthy investors and entrepreneurs, her judgment was no longer questioned. She'd proved herself over and over again to be someone who knew her facts inside out and who could back up every contention with a clear logical answer or solution.

Thousands of dollars and countless man hours went into the preparation of the reports she submitted before permits could be obtained to start a new project. An error was not only costly but could ruin the proposal altogether. It was her awareness of the potential hazards and her determination to avoid them that had won her the reputation of being one of the more reliable and thorough analysts in her field. She had a lot to be proud of, and for the most part, she was. But in this particular case . . .

She loved her work. It suited her disposition perfectly.There were times when she felt she dealt better with facts than with people, that she trusted the words on a piece of paper more than she did human relationships. She liked things to make sense and follow a progressive order. And she found, very often, that people didn't.

Especially in the case of Jeff Warner, but then her whole relationship with him was confusing. If what she felt for him was love, why didn't she feel something special. Why didn't she feel *in* love, like Joe Bonner, Beth, and her mother had assured her she would? Why did people assume that simply because she and Jeff had spent so much time together over the past few years that they were automatically in love and bound for wedded bliss? She and Jeff were friends. They shared many common interests, and they enjoyed each other's company. Granted, there had been a few nights when they had shared some very insipid sex together, but those nights had been fueled by loneliness and a desperate need on both sides to be close to someone. She was sure that Jeff's feelings were no stronger than her own. But what if that was as strong as love ever got?

Leslie sighed and ran her hand back and forth across her brow trying to dispel some of the tension her thoughts had deposited there.

"Does your head still hurt?" Joe asked.

"No."

"Want to sit and rest for a while?"

"If you're tired, we can," she said, refusing to admit that she was dying for a break, too proud to let on that her left arm was sound asleep and that her lower back was throbbing under the weight of her pack.

Joe's eyebrows rose in surprise. "I'm fine," he said, and he kept on walking.

After nearly two hours, Leslie was past the point of pain and almost totally numb.

"I . . . don't . . . whine. I . . . don't . . . whine." She said it over and over in her mind trying to believe it, wanting more than anything to be back in her nice, safe office where she belonged, or as a second alternative, to cry out in misery. Instead she ground her teeth together and watched the dust from the road billow out under her shoes as she flopped them down, step by step, to the rhythm in her head. The thin mountain air ripped at her lungs with every breath, but she kept on walking. She'd rather fall down dead in her tracks than have to cooperate in a kiss with Joe Bonner.

"I'm beat. Let's rest," Joe said suddenly, moving off to the side of the road.

"What?" Leslie asked, stunned.

"I need a break."

"You do?"

Joe nodded. "Don't want to get overtired, you know. Only a fool would walk himself to the point of exhaustion."

There was a reproachful look in his eyes as the zing shot straight up Leslie's spine and registered as a direct hit, but she was in no mood to care. At least she wasn't a whiny fool. She got the distinct impression that it wouldn't matter what she did or how she acted anyway. There would be no pleasing Joe Bonner.

He had already put his heavy load down in the shade along the sloping shoulder of the road, when he turned to see Leslie struggling lamely to remove her own. Mutely he stepped up beside her and untied the knot in the blanket that had slipped down below her bust line. Her skin quivered when his hand accidentally brushed the upper fullness of her breasts, but he didn't seem to notice. Unlike Leslie, he didn't appear to experience the same tingling sensation. In fact he gave every indication that he was perfectly comfortable and totally unaffected standing in her personal space, touching her body, their faces mere inches apart. Leslie, on the other hand, was weak in the knees and fighting to control her irregular breathing. She was afraid to move her head or look into his face for fear of brushing noses with him and prolonging the awkwardness of the moment.

With her pack untied, Joe took it and moved away immediately, leaving Leslie reeling from his sudden withdrawal of his close physical contact, incidental though it was.

Leslie frowned. Get a grip on it, she told herself sternly, you've been out in the sun too long and walked too many miles in his shoes. She rationalized her reactions down to simple physiology. The tingling was blood rushing back into the areas of her body constricted by the weight of her pack. The dizziness and rapid breathing were induced by exhaustion. And a warm rock would look just as strong and comforting right now as his broad chest and thick arms did.

Satisfied and very much relieved with this analysis, Leslie gratefully sank down beside the first large, warm-looking rock she saw.

"Hungry?" Joe asked.

"No. But I am thirsty." She was too tired to eat.

Perched on his own rock several feet away, Joe reached into the cooler and handed her one of the canning jars he'd filled with cool, clear water from the stream earlier. Leslie took it and drank deeply before she screwed the top back on and set the jar down between them.

She lowered her head back to rest it on the rock and closed her eyes. She could almost hear her muscles slowly unwinding, crackling and snapping with tiny bursts of spasmodic pain as they uncurled and became limp.

Joe hadn't missed much of what his traveling companion was going through. He'd seen her shoulders begin to droop. He'd heard her steps begin to drag. And he was sure the bright red flush in her face was caused more from heat and fatigue than overexposure to the sun. She might lean toward stupid sometimes, he thought, but she was a tough little cookie.

"Stubborn little witch," he muttered under his breath, aware that she was probably too far gone to hear him, glad that he'd taken matters into his own hands and finally stopped for the rest she'd refused to ask for.

Joe couldn't resist the unexpected chuckle that rose up within him. This Leslie Rothe was a strange woman. She didn't seem to care that she looked like a refugee from a bag-lady camp or that she was miles into some of the wildest and most treacherous terrain in America without any protection, save maybe himself, if worse came to worst. But she'd walk herself blindly into the ground without a whimper to prove herself and to show him that he'd been wrong about her.

There was a lot of pride and gumption bottled up inside that sleeping pile of rags and warm female flesh. She probably had more dignity than brains, which wasn't always so bad, in his opinion. If she couldn't have her fair share of both, it was just as well she had an overabundance of pride to get her over the rough spots in life. He had to respect that in her at least.

Well, she'd earned her sleep, he decided with a great deal of benevolence. He could afford to feel kindly toward her at the moment, her stubbornness had taken them to within two or three miles of his cabin, and it was early in the afternoon. She could have a short nap, and they'd still be home before total darkness set in. In the meantime there was no law that said he couldn't take a few mental pictures. He liked looking at her. It was better when her deep blue eyes were open and flashing furiously at him, but he'd settle for watching the breeze blow at her dark curls and flutter the jagged hem of her skirt . . . for now.

Leslie woke with a start. She must have been in a deep sleep or not asleep at all, because there were no dreams clouding her mind. She awoke fully, instantly, and could see that nothing had changed while her eyes were closed. In fact, she had the oddest feeling that she was mid-conversation, and it was her turn to respond.

She looked to Joe Bonner for guidance, and he was his usual helpful self. He sat on his rock with an expectant expression on his face, as if waiting for her to answer.

"I'm sorry," she said. "I think I dozed off for a minute. What was your question?"

He looked surprised to hear her admission of weakness and answered in a very civil manner. "I was just asking if you were ready to go?"

With his question asked, he continued to look at her in a curious way that made Leslie very selfconscious. Surely he didn't consider falling asleep synonymous with a complaint. As far as she was concerned, the bet was still on. She hadn't grumbled once—out loud—and she hadn't meant to fall asleep. The least he could do was cut her some slack. She *was* trying.

Slowly she got to her feet. Muscles previously unheard from made their presence known from all parts of her body. They were stiff and ached painfully. The groan that built up in her throat was swallowed quickly as she set her attention on trying to straighten out some of the kinks in her back. All the while she was aware that Joe Bonner was watching her.

"What?" she asked when the strain of his gaze became too great for her to bear.

Joe shook his head as if his thoughts weren't meant for public disclosure but asked, "Do you want more water before we go?"

"Yes, please."

He stood and handed her the jar. Again she drank greedily but had to stop when she felt some of the fluid dripping down her chin. It was then, as she dabbed the sleeve of Joe's shirt across the lower half of her face, that she noticed the groove in the ground near Joe's feet.

It was a long, deep rut, formed as if he'd been dragging the heel of his boot back and forth in the dirt. From the looks of it, he'd been doing just that and for quite some time. Uneasiness grew heavy in her heart. How long had she been asleep?

"It's . . . it's hard to tell the time without a watch," she said, looking up at the sky. "Have we been here long?"

"No."

She glanced in Joe's direction. He was picking up her pack and gave no indication that anything was amiss. He came to her and placed the blanket full of groceries around her shoulders. It felt heavier than before as her tired body protested the familiar burden being settled onto her back.

"It's about four-thirty. We've made good time," he said, tying the blanket ends in a tight knot across her chest.

"How long have we been resting?" she asked, feeling at a distinct disadvantage. Intuitively she knew she'd slept more than just a few minutes—much more—and she wanted to be prepared for whatever Mr. Do-No-Wrong had to say about it.

Joe looked up from his task and met her gaze straight on. "Not long," he said.

The look in his eyes confirmed Leslie's suspicions. They also told her that the man had no intention of teasing her about it. For a brief moment, there was gentleness and understanding in his expression before he lowered his gaze and moved away.

Leslie found this unexpected burst of kindness disconcerting, but she wasn't about to refuse it. She smiled at him when he turned back around, her spirits suddenly buoyant. But when she stepped forward to take up her half of the cooler, she immediately wished she hadn't moved. A sharp, stinging pain set her feet on fire as a cry of agony escaped her.

"What is it?" he asked, alarmed.

Leslie hurt too much to speak. She sat down on the ground and very gingerly removed her shoes. She drew her right foot up into her lap to examine it. It was covered, top and bottom, with large, angry-looking blisters. Some were broken and weeping. Even the air seemed to irritate them and increase the burning pain.

"Oh, geeze," Joe said, his voice full of sympathy.

Leslie looked up into his face. Between the pain impulses bombarding her brain, her mind took the time to register that he was bent down on one knee to investigate the extent of the damage to her feet and that he was being uncharacteristically solicitous of her condition. It was, however, the worried, caring expression she thought she saw in his eyes that was Leslie's undoing.

The blisters were the final blow. Her spirit broken and her life at an all-time low, she was hardly aware of the tears that spilled down her cheeks, leaving a trail of wretchedness in the thin layer of dust and grime acquired during her trek.

"I'm a walking disaster," she said, throwing her hands up in hopelessness. "My whole life is falling down around my ears, and I don't know how to stop it. I don't even know why. I'm completely out of control." She buried her face in her hands and shook her head woefully.

"Oh, no. You're not going to cry are you? I mean, it can't be all *that* bad, can it?"

"It is. And I never cry," she said, and then she sobbed.

"Yes, well, why don't you stop whatever it is you're doing, and we'll talk. The blisters will heal, and I'll bet your sister's wedding went off without a hitch," Joe said, trying to offer her hope, sounding anxious and uncomfortable.

"And what about you?" she asked, looking up at him tearfully. "How long will it take you to recover from the mess I've made of your life? God only knows what I'll do next. I don't even want to think about it. Things keep moving from bad to worse all by themselves. Two weeks is a long time. You could end up dead."

Joe's demeanor grew stern and his green eyes

disapproving. "Oh, spare me, will you? Feeling sorry for poor Leslie isn't going to make things any better. So stop talking all this garbage and help me think of a way to get you to the cabin before nightfall."

Smarting from his insensitivity, Leslie didn't look up when he offered her a clean, neatly folded handkerchief and ordered her to blow her nose. She hadn't consciously been looking for pity, but she couldn't help feeling resentful that Joe Bonner hadn't offered her any. Had a meaner man than Joe Bonner ever been born?

Joe had left Leslie's side while she composed herself, and he now returned to sit Indian-style on the ground facing her. "That's better. Now, let me have a good look at them," he said, holding out his hands.

"Don't bother yourself on my account. Why don't you just go?"

"Come on, poor Leslie. Let Uncle Joe look," he said, mocking her, grinning as if he enjoyed her anger.

Loath to give him more cause to tease her, Leslie thrust her leg out and brought her foot up in front of his face. He patiently and, amazingly enough, gently took hold of her ankle and leg and repositioned them so he could examine her foot.

"Crying and whining are two completely different things, you know," she stated as the thought occurred to her, and then she reconsidered having said it. She shouldn't have brought the subject up at all.

"Not in my book they're not," he said, focusing his eyes on her lips, causing her stomach to somersault. But when she opened her mouth to debate her point, he beat her to the punch. "But I'll make an exception this time. Next time, I'll take my kiss."

"There won't be a next time," she muttered as she watched him grimace at the sight of her battered feet.

"We'll see." Contrary to his words, the careful, tender way he handled her foot led her to believe he had at least an ounce of compassion hidden somewhere. What a strange man he was, she thought. "If it makes you feel any better, more in control again, you can blame these blisters on me. I knew better than to let you walk so far in shoes that didn't fit your feet properly. I didn't think ahead this morning, and I'm sorry for that," he said.

Stunned by his short speech and sincere apology, Leslie didn't know how to reply.

"I wish we'd kept those pieces we cut off your dress," he said, leaning over sideways to pull the cooler closer to them. He then crossed his arms and grabbed the sides of his T-shirt, pulling it up over his head. So in awe of the powerful, broad shoulders and the great expanse of smooth, golden-brown skin before her, Leslie was hardly aware that Joe was speaking again. "This isn't the Red Cross way, I'm sure, but it's the best we can manage right now. We need to keep these clean and dry, so they'll heal."

Suddenly he was ripping his T-shirt.

"What are you doing?" she asked, confused.

"Hopefully I'm going to ease your pain and clean some of the dirt off your feet at the same time." He dunked a large section of his shirt into the melted ice water at the bottom of the cooler. Dripping wet, he then draped the cloth loosely around her inflamed foot.

Leslie couldn't stop the sigh of relief that automatically sprang to her lips. "Ahh. That feels wonderful," she said, her tone euphoric.

Joe smiled and chuckled. "It won't last long, but we might get them numb enough for you to travel at least some of the way without too much pain."

Leslie leaned back on her elbows to enjoy her respite while Joe wrapped her other foot the same way. She felt awful that he'd sacrificed the shirt off his back for her feet, but in that unguarded moment of repose, she was very glad he had—and not because of her blisters. His upper torso was a real treat to look at. The rounded mounds of muscle in his arms and shoulders were a fascinating study in human anatomy, Leslie decided, trying to ignore the squirming sensation low in her abdomen. Irrepressibly her eyes followed the dark trail of hair that curled around his nipples and descended downward, disappearing into the band of his jeans. She blinked disappointedly when her journey ended. She'd seen prettier male faces, but without a doubt, she'd never seen a sexier body.

"Would you like your shirt back, or the coat? It's starting to get cool again," she said as his near nakedness began to make her feel nervous and uncomfortable.

She could have saved the effort of her offer, because when she looked up into his face, she found his gaze riveted to her breasts. In her relaxed position, the shirt had fallen away and left all there was to see exposed. Quickly she sat up and pulled the shirt tightly around her body.

"What's this? A double standard? You can look at my chest, but I can't look at yours?" He tried to look innocent but couldn't keep his lips from bowing upward.

"Do you want the coat or this damned shirt or not?" she asked, her voice almost a snarl as she felt a hot flush working its way up the sides of her neck.

Joe shook his head. "Thanks, but I'll let you know when I get cold, and we'll work something out then." He paused and laughed. "You know, I don't think I've had to take turns wearing a shirt since I was in college."

"You went to college?"

"You sound surprised."

"I am. I mean, I just assumed . . . What did you study?" she asked with interest.

"Journalism."

"Journalism. You're a writer?"

"Yes," Joe said, sounding perturbed with her continued astonishment.

"What do you write? Have you written anything good?" she asked, choosing her words poorly. She wasn't trying to insult him, but she was excited to think that she might have read something he'd written.

But Joe's eyes narrowed, and his posture took on a proud attitude. "Everything I write is good. But if you're asking if I've been published, the answer is yes. Several times in fact. However, if you are wondering if you might have read something of mine, I doubt it. My writing tends to get a little involved."

"Meaning you don't think I read anything heavier than first grade primers, right?" she asked, taking up his role as the insulted intellectual.

"So far you've done nothing to lead me to think otherwise."

Leslie gasped in outrage and frantically searched her mind for a scathing rebuttal. But the truth was, she had been doing some pretty idiotic things since she'd met him. Since before she met him, actually. So how could she fight the truth?

Rather than make some inane remark which would only prove his point, she opted to change the subject entirely. Boldly looking him in the eye, giving him permission to think whatever he liked about her, she asked, "Are you ready to go?"

"Yes. But let's rewrap your feet again first."

When Joe bent to take her foot in his hands, she pulled away, saying, "I can do it."

Joe shrugged indifferently and walked away.

Well, Joe Bonner certainly had been right about one thing, Leslie decided as she soaked his T-shirt in the icy water and reapplied the pieces to her aching feet. This definitely was going to be a long two weeks. What irked her was the fact that she couldn't lay it all at Joe's door. She had never acted so strangely in all her life. It was as if she were functioning on pure emotion. Illogical, irrational, undefinable emotion. She, Leslie Rothe, reacting emotionally. It was like drowning in a desert, very unnatural.

She was feeling sorry for her sister, Beth, for having spent most of her life in this state of ungovernable moodiness, when Joe's activities caught her attention. He had placed their packs and the cooler behind a large boulder and was covering them with dirt and tree limbs and anything else he could find.

"Now what are you doing?" she asked.

"Hiding the food and hoping the animals won't smell it before I come back for it tomorrow," he said without stopping.

"What animals?"

Joe glanced in her direction but went on with his work. "Little forest creatures. Squirrels mostly."

"Are there any bears around here that you know of?"

"Nah. They all moved down to the zoo in Denver," he said facetiously. "But we still have some cute little kitties and some weird looking dogs up here."

Coyotes and mountain lions. Why hadn't she thought of them before? Bears, too, probably. Out of her element didn't exactly describe the way she was feeling. She thought longingly of her nice, safe office. She knew she'd never watch another movie about an extraterrestrial's first visit to earth without having a great deal of empathy for the alien.

"Is that why you want to get there before dark?"

she asked, hoping he'd tell her the animals were never seen in the daylight hours.

"That and the fact that there are no streetlights up here. It gets harder to see where you're going when the sun goes down."

"Oh."

Thinking it better to stay busy rather than dwell on the animals she sensed to be lurking behind nearly everything she looked at, she got to her feet with every intention of helping her companion bury his food. But she didn't need to take that first step to know that she wouldn't get far.

Panic and despair filled her once more. They lodged in her throat as she realized the impossibility of her walking anywhere. Just the pressure of standing on her feet was almost more than she could bear. She sat back down dejectedly and turned her attention to Joe.

She could well imagine what he'd say when he discovered she couldn't walk the rest of the way, but what would he do? Stay and camp out with her until she could travel? Or leave her there for . . . what had he called it last night? Buzzard bait?

She was in the process of wishing she'd been nicer to him, when Joe walked over and held out a hand to help her up. She moved to take it, but at the last minute withdrew her hand.

"It's no use. I can't," she said, defeated.

"You can't what?"

"I can't walk. I'll never make it to your cabin, and I can't blame you for wanting to leave me here, but I think I should warn you that if you do, I'm going to haunt you until the day you die." She finished her impassioned speech on a note of conviction, hoping that she'd impressed him with her supernatural powers.

"Dammit, lady, will you give me a break? I've known

all along you couldn't walk on those damn blisters, and it never once occurred to me to leave you here alone. I don't know why you're so bent on being suspicious of me, but I don't think I deserve it. Or are you suspicious of all men? When you're down in the city and a man holds a door open for you, do you automatically mace him in the face so he won't take your purse?"

"Of course not," she said, feeling guilty—and emotional. How was it that she constantly said things that upset him? "It's just that—"

"Just what? Tell me what I've done," he said, his tone irate, his words rapid and clear.

"Well, it's just that things have been difficult since we met, and I know you don't like me very well and . . ."

"Who said I don't like you? Did I say I don't like you? As I recall, *you* are the one who said you don't like *me*. In fact, you gave me a list of reasons why. But I didn't say I don't like you."

"You mean you do?"

"I didn't say that either," he said, coming up short. He put his hands on his hips and shifted his weight from one foot to the other uncomfortably. "To tell you the truth, I don't know what to think of you. You're the strangest woman I've ever met."

How could Leslie argue with that? She thought she could point out that he, too, was a little strange. But he probably was like that all the time, which would make his behavior normal. Hers was not normal. She was not usually so flighty. Therefore, she deduced, she was easily the stranger of the two of them.

"You're right," she said after a moment of silence. "And I apologize."

"Why?" he asked, suspicious. "Are you still afraid I'll leave you here to die?"

"No. Because I was wrong. Considering the state I've been in, I think you've handled this situation fairly well," she said, speaking in an honest Leslie-like manner.

"High praise indeed," he muttered. He studied her for several long seconds and then finally nodded. "Okay. So, let's go."

"But . . ."

He held up a hand to stop her objection, then put out both hands to assist her up. "Come on, stand up." His voice was lower and softer without his angry tone.

Something very compelling in his eyes asked her to trust him. Their fingers met—hers tentative and unsure, his firm and strong. He gave her a brief, confident smile and pulled her to her feet.

"Okay, good. Now try and stand up on that rock for a second. When I turn around, you climb up on my back," he said.

"Oh, no," she said emphatically as a clear picture formed in her mind. She'd rather have faced the bears in that moment, than have to climb onto his back—his broad, bare sinewy back—and let him carry her for miles while she held on to all that warm, golden skin. The thought mortified her.

"Oh, yes. It's the only way, Leslie." Joe was acting very cavalier about the whole thing. While the simple sound of her name on his lips sent sudden chills up Leslie's spine.

"What about a litter or something?"

"I don't think dragging you is going to be any easier than carrying you, and we'd waste the daylight making it. I don't see that we have any other choice here."

Leslie looked around as if she were hoping to find a wheelchair or, better yet, a taxi. Forlorn, she turned back to Joe, resigned to her fate. Where were fairy godmothers when you really needed them, she wondered in her desperation.

"Come on, cheer up. I'll bet you haven't had a piggyback ride since you were a little girl," Joe said, laughing at her discomfort.

"There's a good reason for that. I'm a lot bigger now. You'll end up with bilateral hernias."

"Come on. Come on," he said, growing impatient. "If I give you more time, you'll have a whole list of reasons not to do this. Now, get up there."

He helped Leslie onto the flat edge of a nearby rock, which made her nearly a foot taller than he. Then he turned, drawing her arms around his neck as he went. "Okay, now wrap those nice long legs of yours around my waist so I'll have something to hold on to." When she had no choice but to comply, he hiked her up onto his back and gave her a prefatory swat on her bottom saying, "And don't drag your tail, or you'll slow us down."

Leslie had never felt so completely unraveled. Where was her simple, logical life? Where was her calm, unemotional disposition? Wrapping herself around Joe's big, hard body made her feel like she'd entered a fifth dimension. His long, dark hair brushed against her cheek and tickled fantasies not in her usual repertoire. Even the not so clean and overworked smell of him was somehow erotic and made her muscles jumpy. She had to remind herself that this wasn't normal behavior, that she needed to be embarrassed and feel like an utter fool. Still all she could think about was running her hands over his smooth, warm skin.

"Talk to me," Joe said after a while, his words rushing out on a labored breath.

"What about?"

"Anything. You. What you do. It'll make the time go faster if I'm distracted."

"Oh. Well, I'm a research analyst. I work a lot with computers. I gather facts and data on a specific subject and develop an hypothesis about it. It's like putting a puzzle together. I take a whole bunch of little pieces of information and put them together to make a clear, overall picture."

"That's amazing," Joe said.

"It is. And it's a lot of fun too. I enjoy it very much."

"No, I meant it's amazing that you do that. I guess I just hadn't pictured you doing something so detailed and involved."

Peering over his shoulder, Leslie cast him a sidelong glance and held her breath as her pride bristled. Suddenly, riding on this man's back and listening to him gasp and groan didn't seem so bad. "Just exactly what did you have me pictured as?" she asked in a too-sweet voice.

"I don't know. I guess, at first, I thought you were a model or something because of what you were wearing. I thought maybe you'd been on a shoot up here and had gotten lost. But once you explained about the dress, I didn't think anymore about it."

"So why are you so amazed that I'm a research analyst?"

"I'm not amazed exactly. Just surprised."

"That's basically the same thing," she said.

Joe turned his head and tried to look at her. Then he laughed. "I am so tempted to tell you to get off my back," he said with a chuckle in his voice. "But instead, I'll just ask if you're trying to pick another fight with me?"

"Maybe."

"All right, then. I'm about as amazed that you're a research analyst as you were when you found out I went to college. How's that?"

Leslie fell momentarily silent. "That makes us even then. I'm sorry."

"Let's rest a second," he said. Carefully he released and lowered her feet to the ground behind him. Her knees felt like wet spaghetti, but Joe was there to help her sit down. When he finally got around to tending to himself, twisting and stretching his aching back muscles, he didn't seem to notice that he had Leslie's rapt attention.

Her own body began to tingle and squirm as she watched him. Her mind conjured up an image of thick, powerful arms encircling her, of a back bending forward and curving around to protect her. A sigh escaped her, and the vision vanished, leaving Leslie to wonder where it had come from.

When Joe suddenly turned back to her with a grin on his face and a bemused sparkle in his eyes, her heart flipped over and began to pump frantically. Seeing pleasure on his face did the strangest things to her.

"You know, for a couple of real smart people, we've sure as hell made a mess of things," he said with great amusement.

"We certainly have," she agreed, in a much more serious tone.

Five

Joe and Leslie reached the end of their journey in relative amicability. They hardly spoke. Joe seemed to be concentrating heavily on taking one forward step after another, while Leslie fought to keep her "tail" from dragging. She couldn't remember ever being so weary.

The aching stiffness in her arms, back, and legs made the pain in her feet almost forgettable. She could well imagine how Joe felt and allowed gratitude to slip into her heart.

He turned off the main logging road and began to ascend a slow upgrade. Leslie heard him groan, not in exhaustion this time but in relief.

"Are we close?" she asked, anxious to have this part of her ordeal come to an end.

"Mm," was his affirmative response.

She guessed it to be early evening. It was still light out, but the shadows of the trees were very long and the sun was no longer heating them. She felt not the slightest compunction to offer Joe his shirt back, though, because she knew he didn't need it.

The front of the shirt was the only thing that separated their bodies, and it was soaked with his perspiration. Her hands could feel and would sometimes slip on the clammy warmth of his skin. Even the air she breathed, so close to his neck and the side of his face, was humid and scented with the evidence of his exertion. The shirt was the last thing he needed.

Funny man, Joe Bonner. So cold and aloof one minute—like he was earlier that morning—and so willing to help, so kind and gentle and friendly the next. She never quite knew what he was thinking or what he'd do next. But all along she was aware that there was something very special and thrilling about being close to this particular human being.

She was too tired to be excited sexually, and the uncommon feeling went much deeper than that anyway. It was more like a bonding, an exclusive link between them. It was something neither of them had asked for or particularly wanted, but it was there nevertheless. It was like the connection between two people who had taken on an insurmountable obstacle together and won, or had fought and suffered together and lived to tell about it. Of course, in this instance, it seemed to Leslie that she had done most of the suffering and Joe had done most of the fighting, but overall, she'd come to know that she could trust him.

That was it. The bond. She trusted Joe Bonner, and he accepted that faith. With this peculiar revelation, Leslie realized that she'd never truly trusted another person outside her family before. How odd. And why hadn't she? Her life hadn't been a succession of traumatic disappointments. And why now? Why Joe Bonner of all people?

A panicky feeling crept into her consciousness and filled her mind with question marks. And questions without answers made her very nervous. Suddenly all she wanted to do was put some distance between herself and Joe Bonner.

"Maybe I could walk from here."

"Maybe you might have to, but let's see how far I can get you. Your feet are in such bad shape," he said, reestablishing a firmer hold around her thighs, his breathing deep and ragged.

She looked up, and over his shoulder she saw it. It was a small wooden structure with three windows and a door on the near side and a stone chimney visible on the end closest to them. It didn't look much bigger than her own living room and kitchen put together. It was nothing to shout about, but that's exactly what she did, as if it were a castle.

"We made it, Mr. Bonner. Look. That's it, isn't it? Oh, Lord, I've never been so happy to see a place before," she said exuberantly.

"Leslie! Be still," he said, staggering under her excitement. When he was under control again, he asked, "And when are you going to start calling me Joe?"

"I don't know. When you feel like a Joe to me, I guess," she said guilelessly, some of the old honest and logical Leslie asserting itself.

"Oh. That's interesting. And what's the difference between a Joe and a Mr. Bonner?"

"One's a stranger, and the other isn't."

Joe stopped ten feet from the front of the house and craned his neck to look at her. When he could see that she wasn't joking, he sighed deeply, took the remaining few steps to his front door, and lowered Leslie onto the small front porch. Then he turned to her with a frown of disbelief on his face and asked, "After all we've been through in the last twenty-four hours, *I'm* still a stranger to you?"

"Technically, yes," she said, taken aback and on the defensive again by his display of irritation. "I think you've been very nice to put up with me. But I know nothing about you except your name and profession and that you went to college somewhere."

Joe was quiet at first. His lively green eyes searched steadily for something in the expression on her face or in her eyes or around her mouth, because they covered all those places. Finally, almost in disgust, he nodded and said, "Mr. Bonner suits me just fine, lady." He turned on his heel and started to walk away.

Obviously she had hurt his feelings, and she was instantly sorry for that. She hadn't meant to. Her mother was right, she had no tact. She lacked a sensitivity to other people's feelings. She also had a lack of interest in the world around her—or she had until the day before. She wondered when she had become so self-absorbed or if she'd always been that way, a victim of some sort of mutation in her emotional makeup.

She wanted to call out to Joe, to apologize or tell him she had only been joking. But she didn't want to lie to him either. She threw up her hands in helplessness. Somehow she'd have to find a way to mend this new breach between them. She actually wanted to this time. She felt an odd craving to be able to call Mr. Bonner, Joe.

"Where are you going?" she called out after him, needing to assure herself that he was going to return.

"To the shed for firewood," he said shortly.

"Oh. Would it be all right if I used your bathroom, then? I'm dying to take a bath."

In slow motion, Joe turned to face her. There was an evil little smirk dancing about his lips and his eyes were filled with pure devilment. "That would be a neat trick if you could swing it."

"There's no bathtub in your bathroom?" Joe shook his head. "I don't mind. A shower will be just as nice."

"And just as good a trick," he said, pointing to an extremely small shedlike configuration off to the side and some distance from the cabin.

"Then what . . ." Leslie's voice trailed off as she realized the truth. A feeling that she knew must be very close to hysteria seized her. "An outhouse? You don't have a bathroom? You drag me all the way up this damned mountain, put blisters on my feet, and humiliate me every chance you get, and you don't even have a bathroom? How am I supposed to take a bath and wash my hair, not to mention soak my feet, if you don't have a bathroom?" she said, her voice rising higher and higher as she came close to tears.

In keeping with what Leslie had come to know as his totally illogical and obnoxious character, Joe laughed merrily. "That's it! That's what I've been waiting for," he said. He did a funny little two-step in the dirt and then advanced on her with long, purposeful strides. He swept a startled and angry Leslie into his arms and pressed her body close, molding it to fit his perfectly. He was grinning triumphantly. He was so close she could see the pupils of his eyes dilating and constricting as he cast his gaze over her face and down to her lips. "You see. I knew if you really set your mind to it, you'd find something to whine about. It's time to pucker up, sweetheart."

Leslie glared at him. She could feel his heart hammering. . . . No, it was her own heart hammering wildly in her chest. She was excited and anxious and her agitation was upsetting her stomach. "But this isn't fair. Bathrooms are important," she objected weakly.

"A deal's a deal, Leslie," he said as he traced her lips with his tongue, his voice low and intimate. "I want my kiss."

There was a huge lump in her throat as she tried to swallow away her nervousness and what was left of her fury. She wasn't crazy about the idea of having to admit that she'd lost the bet, but the idea of proving something else to this man became suddenly very appealing. She'd show him snooty. She'd show him someone who'd never been in love. She'd show him just how atypical a female she was.

With her courage bolstered by her pride, she liberated the resistance in her body and melted against him. Her lips brushed his, teasing and enticing. She nudged his nose with hers and tilted her head to take better aim at the target area. Slowly, meticulously she took his bottom lip between her teeth and sipped at it gently.

She felt the man's body grow tense and heard him draw in a deep hissing breath as she continued to use every sensuous trick she'd ever discovered to worry his libido. Her fingertips moved like feathers over his bare chest. She felt his muscles quiver and laughed wickedly in her heart. When he groaned and deepened the kiss, taking her possessively, his arms tightening about her like a vice, she knew a moment of terror and panic and briefly wished she hadn't tested his restraint. But it was a short-lived moment. She knew a feeling of dizzy breathlessness as he sapped the air right out of her. Her own muscles grew weak and tingled helplessly as his hands roamed over her body, looking for an entrance into her clothes.

When his lips left hers to trail slowly down her neck toward her open shirt front, her heart skipped several beats and a sense of fear rose up to help clear her mind. She took a staggered step away from him and looked straight into his eyes when they opened. Quite clearly, he was as shaken as she that the payoff to their bet had gone so far and been so kinetic. Their amazement was mutual and quite awkward.

His gaze was intense and thoughtful for several

long moments before he spoke. "Cornell. I went to Cornell," he said. Then, abruptly, he released her and walked away. But before he got too far, he turned to her again, saying, "You want to make any more bets with me?"

"I don't think so," she said, still a little short of air.

"Too bad, because I already know what I want when you lose again. And I gotta tell you, Leslie, I truly admire a loser who pays up with such enthusiasm."

"Humph," was her disdainful response as she tried to appear indifferent, which wasn't too hard when he began to laugh at her haughtiness.

He continued to laugh and seemed quite pleased with himself as he walked around the end of the cabin and out of sight. A slow, even growl of rage erupted from Leslie. She wanted to stomp her feet but recalled their condition in time. Great kisser or not, the man was a pompous pig.

In frustration she turned to the cabin. No longer a castle, the structure now fell sadly short of her definition of rustic. In her present frame of mind, it didn't look much better than a cave.

The door squeaked endearingly as she opened it and hobbled through. Joe Bonner seemed to have a place for everything and everything seemed to be in its place. To her left there was a vintage 1950s overstuffed sofa and easy chair, with wooden crates for end tables. Beyond them was the fireplace. There was a cooking area on her right with a dinette table and three chairs set out in the middle of the floor. And on the far wall, facing her, was another table and the fourth chair to the dinette set. On this table rested a small personal computer with a pile of papers and several books, stacked according to size, beside it.

"No bathroom, but he's got a damn computer,"

she muttered as she automatically looked to see the make of the instrument. Well acquainted with computers, she recognized it as a top-of-the-line battery-operated model and knew it to be expensive. At least his taste in high-tech equipment was good.

To the left of the computer table on the same side of the room was a bed covered with a patchwork comforter, a large wooden chest of drawers, and a nail in the wall from which he'd hung a suit and three neatly pressed dress shirts on hangers. Actually, as her anger began to ebb away, the cabin began to look somewhat nicer. Joe Bonner, it appeared, was a neat and tidy person. There were book shelves and cabinets in every available space. All were packed neatly and to capacity. There were even pictures on the pine-paneled walls, scenes of the Old West not to Leslie's liking, but then she didn't have to live here long, did she?

No, in a calmer state of mind and with Joe Bonner nowhere in sight, the cabin was quite homey. Well satisfied, she looked at her surroundings with an air of mild acceptance. In fact, as far as she could tell, there was only one little problem with it aside from the fact that there was no bathroom. There was only one room and one bed—both of which could lend themselves to some very sticky situations when dealing with a lunatic like Joe Bonner, she decided.

For example, who was going to get the bed and who was going to sleep in the woodshed? Not king or even queen size, the bed was just an average bed. But to Leslie it looked like a small square of heaven. She approached it in a state of reverence and crawled into the middle of the mattress. Firm and soft at once, the bed accepted her weight and encouraged her to lie back and get comfortable.

Nothing in her life had felt so good. She flung her

arms out across the bed, her eyes closed automatically, and she exhaled a deep sigh of bliss. She became vaguely aware that Joe was stomping around on the porch outside the door. She wondered briefly if he'd be warm enough in the shed. Then, from far away she heard him call out to her. She answered but the response never reached her lips.

"Oh, no you don't," he said, although his voice was muffled and distant. "Don't even think about getting comfortable on my bed. You're sleeping on the couch. It's too short for me and . . ."

Slowly, Leslie entered that time and space that was only half reality and half something else, that gap in consciousness between deep sleep and wakefulness that she usually lingered in and enjoyed. She tried to change positions but found her muscles stiff and cramped. Extending herself out in all directions, she stretched and twisted, lessening some of her discomfort and coming more fully awake. When she could move with relative ease, she rolled over and came face to face with Joe Bonner.

He'd been awake for some time it was easy to see. He looked very alert and very displeased. He came up on one elbow and seemed oblivious to the effect his bare chest had on Leslie's nervous system, as he looked down at her in earnest. "As I was saying, this bed is mine. From now on *you* sleep on the couch."

It may have been the way he said it, or it simply may have been the fact that it was indeed a new day and not an extension of the last two, or it may have been because Leslie was well rested and didn't feel at all like an emotional basket case, but she took instant exception to his order.

"You know," she said, looking him calmly in the eye, ignoring the hair and the tight brown circles on his chest, "I'm getting a little sick of this attitude of yours. I appreciate all you did for me yesterday, and I appreciate your taking me into your home, but that doesn't mean I'm going to lie here and let you boss me around and brow beat me for the next two weeks . . . or however long it is. You can have your damned bed and—how come you're clean?" she asked, abruptly ending her heated speech when she noticed that he was clean and shaven.

"*I* took the time to take a bath last night before I went to bed so I wouldn't get the sheets all dirty. Which is also why I just threw a blanket over you instead of undressing you and putting you to bed," he said, grinning as he watched her becoming shocked and pink cheeked at the thought that she'd left herself that vulnerable to him again. "That, and I knew you'd have me for breakfast if I even dared to touch you without permission," he admitted, even as he audaciously splayed his hand across her waist, resting his thumb in the valley between her breasts. Even through the material of her gown, she could feel the heat of his touch. It spread through her slowly like sweet, warm honey.

She brushed his hand away as she would a pesky fly. "That's very good. At least you're not unteachable."

"Don't get snooty again, or I won't tell you where you can take a bath." He was looking smug, and Leslie wanted very much to slap him.

"Would you please tell me where I might take a bath?" she asked, smiling stonily.

"Certainly." Thinking he was as naked below the waist as he was above it, Leslie gasped when he threw back the covers and got out of bed. When he stood there smirking at her, reading her thoughts and adjusting the tie string on his pajama bottoms, she once again had to curb the urge to do him bodily harm. "You can wear the tops tonight, if you want. Or do you sleep in the nude?"

Quickly checking under the covers to be sure all was as it should be, she jumped out of bed and stood scowling at him. "Are you going to show me where I can bathe or not?"

"If you'll allow me some privacy so I can get dressed, I will," he said, his tone intimating that it didn't matter if she left or not, he was about to get naked anyway. She turned to leave, but his voice stopped her. "How are your feet this morning?"

Oddly enough she hadn't thought of them yet. She looked down to find them cleaner than the night before and far less inflamed. When she looked up at Joe, he shrugged. "I cleaned them up a little last night. We can't afford to have them get infected." He paused briefly, then added, "That's also when I decided to leave you sleeping on my bed. I figured anyone who could just lie there with her eyes closed while someone poured water over the open blisters on her feet was either dead or dead tired."

"I was tired. Thank you." There was a queer feeling in the pit of her stomach as she thought about Joe Bonner, at least as tired as she had been, taking the time to clean her feet so they wouldn't get infected. It was a nice thing to do, and she was about to tell him so, when he tossed two dark objects in her direction.

"You can wear these," he said. They were brown leather moccasins with a soft fur lining. Worn and more his size than hers, they'd be perfect to wear until her feet healed. Again, she felt a warm, beholden sort of feeling toward the man and wanted to express it. But when she looked up at him again, he was untying the string of his pajamas and smiling licentiously. "Pretty soon it'll be your turn to show and tell."

Grabbing up a blanket, she wrapped it tightly around her and went out to stand on the front porch. It was a relief to get away from him. She disliked the feeling of being his sole source of entertainment. She found him much more appealing when he was being kind and sympathetic and heroic. The trouble was, she never knew what he was going to do next.

It wasn't long before he walked out into the cool, crisp morning air to join her. He was dressed much like he had been the day they met—jeans, T-shirt, and a blue-plaid flannel shirt. She followed him around the side of the cabin, and there, leaning up against it was a portable bathtub. Oblong, perhaps four or five feet long and two and a half feet wide, it was made of some sort of hard plastic and didn't at all appear to be a luxury item. However, it would suit its purpose, Leslie decided.

"Inside or out?" Joe wanted to know, as if she knew what he was talking about. When she simply looked at him with a bland expression on her face, he explained. "Do you want to take your bath out here or in the cabin?"

Fool, she called him, from the back of her mind. In the cabin, of course, unless . . . "Where will you be?"

"I'm going back after the food, so you'll have the whole place to yourself."

"Inside, then. What's this?" she asked, looking over a large patch of tilled and well-cultivated ground.

"My garden."

"I see," she said, taking in the fact that it was barren, wondering when he planned to plant it. Even a city slicker knew gardens didn't plant themselves. And it was getting late in the season.

Joe carried the tub in for her and placed it in front of the fire. He apparently had anticipated her needs, as there was a large kettle of water already steaming on the stove. He told her it would take two or three kettlefulls depending on how hot she wanted the bath water, and to be sure to mix in some cold or she'd burn her little fanny.

Keeping a tight rein on her temper, she thanked him and assured him she could carry on. But instead of going straight to the door and leaving, he walked over to one of the cabinets and opened it. He drew out first a double-barreled shotgun and then, apparently reconsidering his choice, replaced it and took out a very lethal looking pistol.

"Here, you might need this. Do you know how to use it?" he asked.

"No. I hate guns."

"Well, while you're here alone you might want to develop a liking for one. You don't have to shoot anything. In fact, I'd prefer it if you didn't try to. You can shoot it off over your head or into the ground if you need to. The sound will scare most animals away. But if you aim and hit one, this won't kill it. It'll only wound it and make it mad. Understand?"

"Is it really necessary? I mean, well, wouldn't a scream do just as well?"

He seemed to consider her question while he checked to see if there were bullets in the gun. Glancing at her, he then checked the aim of the gun, saying, "I don't think so. I guess I could stay, but like I said, I planned to go back to get the rest of our food while you took your bath. But if you want to take the risk that I might peek at you while you're bathing, well, who am I to argue?" His careful expression told her he'd definitely peek.

Torn, Leslie sought an alternative. There didn't seem to be one. Given the choice between having to carry a gun, which was abhorrent to her, and having to put up with this fool of a man trying to catch a cheap thrill by peeking at her, her decision came fairly easily. "Okay. Peek if you want, but I'm not going to use that gun."

Joe frowned. "Really? You hate guns that much?" When she only nodded, he continued contritely. "I was hoping you'd take the gun and save me the time. But if you really feel that strongly, I'll wait for you. There're clean towels in the bottom dresser drawer."

"Thank you." She got the feeling that whatever it was that he was saving his time for was important to him. So she asked him about it while they waited for more water to boil.

"I have a deadline I'm trying to meet. I lost a day and a half with the accident, and I was hoping to make it up today," he explained.

He wasn't accusing or blaming her for anything, but then he didn't have to. Leslie was packing around enough guilt these days to saddle herself with being the cause of the strife in the Middle East. She wished she could help him. "Look. How likely is it, exactly, that an animal would come anywhere near me today? I haven't seen or heard anything bigger than a squirrel or a rabbit in the past two days."

"The chances aren't great. You might see a deer or something, but the way our luck's been going, I'd rather not leave you unprotected."

"What would you say if I told you I was feeling very lucky today?"

"I'd say you were lying and trying to be nice." He smiled at her in a way that was meant to be friendly and appreciative. She looked away quickly. Her reactions to his smiles were not logical, and that made her uncomfortable.

"Really, I think I'll be fine if you want to go ahead and go. I'll take a quick bath, and I'll keep the door locked. I won't even leave the cabin. I know I haven't exactly proved it to you yet, but there are people who actually think of me as being quick witted and able to take care of myself."

"There are?" His words were insulting, but his expression was teasing.

"Yes," she said smiling back, trying to sound confident as she envisioned herself fighting off a hungry puma with a stick. "There really are. And I do feel much better today. I think you should go."

"Are you sure?" She nodded reassuringly. Joe frowned as if he wasn't at all certain. Finally he sighed and agreed. "Okay. It shouldn't take long. A couple of hours tops."

Joe left, and the cabin began to creek and groan loudly as if it missed his presence. Leslie, of course, didn't miss him a bit. It was only natural for her to feel a little skittish, out in the middle of nowhere, in an unfamiliar cabin, sitting in a strange little bathtub, with all kinds of vicious animals slinking around outside the door. She felt just as fidgety when Joe was around. In a slightly different way, naturally. But what it boiled down to was six of one and half a dozen of the other.

Amazingly enough, it wasn't long before the warm water took effect and began to soothe her aching muscles and jangled nerves. She submerged herself totally in an effort to cleanse herself of the dirt of the last two days. Joe's soap on a rope smelled manly, as if it just had sailed in from one of the seven seas, but Leslie didn't care. The lather felt wonderful, so wonderful, she washed her hair twice with it.

Feeling fresh and uplifted, she got out of the tub and wrapped herself in a large yellow towel. She felt like a new woman. Well, not exactly like a new woman, more like the old Leslie with a few new insights. She didn't have the answers she'd been looking for, and there was still the matter of the mountain to come to terms with, but there was something else too. A strength that comes from inside when you least expect it. A desire to go on when things look hopeless. A knowledge that for every question or problem there is a suitable solution, if one kept searching for it. And looking for answers is what Leslie did best.

Wistfully she wished Joe were back. She wanted to share her good feelings with him, show him that she wasn't always the woebegone fool he'd picked up in the woods two days ago. Leslie sighed. Boldly she opened the front door and looked out at the new day. Ponderosa pines towered over her, the aspen fluttered in the breeze, even the little blue flowers that trailed along the ground seemed bigger and brighter and more beautiful than they had the day before. Vaguely she wondered just where she was. Would the construction of her company's project extend this far into the mountains? She couldn't remember, but it was most certainly going to be the first thing she looked up when she got home. Joe would hunt her down and draw blood if she were responsible for destroying his hideaway. Unless . . . Was there still a way to put a stop to the project? Some way to right her wrong?

Leslie was in her problem-solving mode when she reentered the cabin. First things first, she decided, dropping her towel on the floor. She couldn't save a mountain if she wasn't dressed for it.

Leslie felt she could claim a thorough and intimate knowledge of Joe's entire wardrobe. She could attest to the fact that he'd had no women visitors, or if he had, he let them all go home with their underwear on. Having to choose from among the huge selection of white T-shirts and jeans she found had been tough. So she chose the ones on top and turned her attention to the flannel shirts. She picked a red one because it was that sort of day. Joe's jeans were quite big in the waist, and he apparently had only one belt—the one he had on. Feeling that perhaps it was being put to its best use in keeping Joe's pants in place, she opted to use one of his ties. Consciously, she picked out the ugliest one she could find. It was red with weird little emblems dotted all over it. It was also on the bottom, closest to the nail on which the ties hung, which lead her to believe Joe seldom wore it and that he wouldn't object to her using it for a belt.

Coffee was next on her list. She definitely was going to miss her coffee maker in the next two weeks, but the little tin pot and the wood-burning stove would have to do for now. It was while she was waiting for the coffee to brew that she found the pistol Joe had left on one of the wooden crates.

It was an evil-looking instrument. Cold, black, metallic, just looking at it sent a shiver up her spine. Still, she disliked admitting that she was afraid of it. Grudgingly she had to concede it had a useful purpose—scaring off large animals. What if Joe ran into some fierce wild beast on his way back from the outhouse some night, and she couldn't lift a finger to help him, she wondered. She owed it to him, after all he'd done for her, to at least be able to shoot the gun if an emergency arose, she concluded.

She reached out and picked up the pistol by its handle then laid it back down again. If she was going to shoot a gun, she was going to shoot the loudest one. She walked over to the cabinet Joe had opened before, and with great care and trepidation, removed the double-barreled shotgun. Assuming it to be loaded, as the pistol had been when Joe checked it, she was careful to keep it aimed at the floor until she got it out of the cabin.

Leslie was surprised that it was heavier than it

looked. Why anyone would choose to use it in a bank robbery puzzled her, because it was very awkward to handle. Joe had said that her best targets would be the sky and the ground, and taking into consideration the weight of the thing, she felt the ground to be her best bet.

Careful to move her feet out of the way, she put the butt of the rifle under her right arm. Supporting the gun with her left hand, she extended her right index finger to the trigger. She paused to take several deep breaths, telling herself this was something she had to learn for Joe's sake. Then she closed her eyes and squeezed the trigger. It didn't move. She tried it again with the same results. It didn't make sense to her. Joe wouldn't keep a gun that didn't work in his cabin.

Upon closer inspection, it didn't take her long to find the little safety lock and release it. Repeating her previous steps, she regathered her courage and pulled the trigger again. The sound was not only deafening, it was terrifying. But it was the force of the shot being put to the ground that was so powerful; it knocked Leslie clean off her feet, throwing her backward to land flat on her back, winded and stunned.

For several long minutes she lay there sucking in air, aware of the throbbing ache in her right arm and shoulder and wondering what good she would be in the event of an emergency if she couldn't stand and shoot a gun at the same time. She was just about to get back on her feet and try it again, when she heard Joe's panic-stricken voice calling out to her.

Six

Leslie knew she should have gotten up and made it clear that she was unharmed. She wanted to get up, but she was curious to see what Joe would do. Was his alarm due to the fact that someone was hurt? Or due to the fact that he thought *she* was hurt? Playfully, she kept her eyes closed and didn't twitch a muscle.

First she heard and then she felt the rhythm of Joe's steps as they raced toward her. He called her name twice before he reached her side.

"Dammit to hell! I knew it. I should never have left you here alone. Leslie? Leslie, can you hear me?" he asked, his voice unsteady and full of fear. "Les?"

She could feel his hands on her shoulders as they gently moved up to examine her neck and the back of her head. They came down again, over her arms and ribs, then quickly to her legs.

"Where are you hurt? Oh, wake up and tell me where you hurt," he pleaded, growing more distressed by the second.

Perhaps this wasn't such a good idea, after all, Leslie pondered, while she relished the feel of his hand on her cheek as he gently pushed her hair away from her face. She got the distinct impression that if she suddenly came to life right now, Joe would surely kill her for deceiving him. She opened her right eye just a smidgen to get a look at the expression on his face. Even though her vision was hazy, she could tell he was extremely upset.

"Hmm, I don't see any bleeding," he said, passing his hands over her shoulders again. "I hope you're not bleeding internally." He sounded horrified by the very idea.

His hands moved down along her ribs and more intimately across her pelvis to the juncture of her legs. Slowly, they traveled upward palpating her abdomen and still higher until they curved around her breasts. Her unbuttoned outer shirt had fallen away, leaving only the thin T-shirt as a barrier between her and Joe's searching hands. Her heart beat painfully in her throat when his fingers lingered to fondle and caress. He teased the hardening peaks with his thumbs, and air caught in her lungs. She began to feel truly faint as he continued to arouse every nerve ending in her body until it stood up and screamed with need.

"Ah . . ." she groaned loudly as she struggled to sit up and end the game. Fortunately, her right shoulder really did hurt, or she'd have come up too quickly and blown the whole act. She'd have to be more careful, she reminded herself. "Where am I?"

"Where you belong, sweetheart. Flat on your back," Joe said in a saccharine voice, his anxiety subdued too rapidly, much to Leslie's dismay. Brave enough to open only one eye, she saw that he had leaned back on his legs and was watching her, undeceived. So much for the great new day, she thought fatalistically.

With both eyes open, she hung her head in shame, unable to look him in the eye, until she remembered what he'd done. "You were pawing me! You knew all along I wasn't hurt, and you took advantage of me," she blurted out, incensed.

Joe's mouth dropped open at her brazen outburst. "You've got a nerve," he shouted right back. "After what you did to me? Scaring me like that? You're lucky that's all I did. I ought to roll you over and spank you."

Leslie's eyes narrowed as her rage grew out of control. "You try it, and I'll kill you," she said, wrapping her fingers around the shotgun that still lay beneath her right hand. It barely was an inch off the ground when Joe's eyes lowered to the gun wrapped tightly in her fist. His gaze returned to meet and hold hers with a penetrating stare. Joe didn't move a muscle. He sat there watching her calmly as if he knew she wouldn't take aim and couldn't pull the trigger.

He was right. Leslie's mind took a step forward, and she saw herself holding a deadly weapon, aimed straight at another human being. The sight was nauseating, her body convulsed at the horror of it. She laid the rifle back down on the ground. "I'm sorry," she said in a soft voice, this time she was truly ashamed.

"So am I." Joe's deep, harsh voice was so understanding and sincere that she couldn't help looking up at him. He smiled at her. "You scared me. I wanted to teach you a lesson."

"It was a bad joke on my part. I've learned my lesson." She laughed softly at herself, and said, "Actually, I should have known better. I never was very good at pretending. Even when I was a little girl."

Joe was smiling at her. His expression took on a wistfulness as his gaze roamed over her face. "I'll bet you were a cute little girl."

Under his intense scrutiny and unaccustomed to his softhearted words, Leslie felt selfconscious and warm all over. Their gazes locked. In that instant, there was a vague connection made between them. He stated a fact, and she accepted it and agreed with it. But neither of them would acknowledge it as they looked away in denial.

Joe cleared his throat loudly, then addressed her point blank. "What the hell were you shooting at anyway? I told you to use the handgun if you needed to. You idiot. You're lucky you didn't break your arm with that shotgun."

She wanted to tell him about a pack of wolves in an effort to maintain his caring attitude, but it wasn't exactly her style. Try as she might to follow her mother's advice, lying just never seemed to work for her. "I wasn't shooting at anything. I thought I should at least try to shoot a gun in case of an emergency. I thought this gun would be louder."

"Bigger is better, huh?"

"Well, that's what I was hoping."

"Can you stand up? Are you feeling okay?"

"Yes."

"All right then, come here."

Leslie got to her feet as she watched Joe pick up the shotgun and check to see if the second round was still in place. He motioned for her to come to him, and when she was within touching distance, he took her arm and pulled her even closer.

"Now," he said, drawing her into his arms so that she was facing away from him. "I'll show you the correct way to do it, if you really want to learn how." He put the gun to her shoulder, making a point of telling her that it didn't go in her armpit. He used a lot of technical talk to tell her, in essence, that if she planned to shoot a gun bigger than the size of her foot, not to aim it directly into the ground, to angle it more, or the backlash would knock her down every time.

Leslie didn't particularly want and wasn't at all interested in this lesson on how to handle a shotgun. She had no intention of ever touching a gun again as long as she lived. If an emergency arose, she'd think of something else to do. But, she wasn't about to tell Joe. She liked the feel of his arms around her as he held her close, the way they brushed against her when he moved. She liked watching his big, rough hands as they took hers and showed her where to put them on the rifle. And there was no denying the warm, tingling sensation she felt when his legs pressed against the back of hers and his chest adjusted itself to conform to her back.

She almost giggled with delight when he put his cheek to hers and tried to show her how the sight worked. He could have repeated that specific part of the lesson several times, and she wouldn't have minded.

"Now then, all you have to do is keep that branch lined up with the sight on the end of the barrel, and pull the trigger. And don't close your eyes, or you'll lose your aim. Ready?" Leslie nodded. "Keep your legs spread apart, or you'll be back on your fanny again."

There was a laughing quality in his voice that she took instant exception to and very naturally turned her head to glare at him. Her nose brushed his cheek, and their eyes met and held for a long tense moment of appraisal.

"Would you like to make a wager on your hitting that branch?" he asked, leaving no doubt as to what the stakes would be.

"I don't think so."

"Afraid you'll lose again?"

"Yes."

"It's bound to happen eventually," he said, almost like a warning in her ear. "Wouldn't you just as soon get it over with than have to live with the anticipation that much longer?"

"What anticipation?" she asked, looking away, making an elaborate gesture of squaring her shoulders and bracing her legs as she took careful aim at the branch.

"The anticipation of knowing that eventually you and I are going to make love. And don't tell me you haven't thought about it."

"I haven't thought about it." Well, not in so many words, she added mentally. Her hands grew moist, and her heart was racing as he continued to talk softly, intimately in her ear.

"I know you have. Look, Leslie. See how well our bodies fit together? I noticed it the other night when you spent the whole night in my arms. We'll do that again soon. Only this time you won't be sleeping." Leslie's muscles grew taut, and her nerves became excited. She flexed and extended her trigger finger, trying to keep her concentration focused on the tree limb. "It'll be glorious, Leslie. I'm already looking forward to touching your soft, smooth skin again. To kissing you again. To finding softer places to touch and secret places to kiss, that—"

The shotgun went off with a resounding clap that seemed to go on forever. When Leslie opened her eyes, she was amazed to find the branch gone. Triumphantly she turned on Joe. "There. Happy now?"

"Are you? You're the one who wouldn't bet." His green eyes were sparkling proudly. He'd been goading her, she realized instantly. Saying all those horrible things so she'd try harder to make the shot. She began to seethe.

"Ah, ah, ah. Don't get mad now. If you're a very good girl, it may just happen yet," he said, tapping her nose lightly with his index finger. "And next time you decide to play dead, don't try to peek. It makes your eyelashes flutter."

Leslie gasped. He released his instructor's hold on her and took the rifle from her hands. "Since you're feeling so spunky today, you can help me carry all that food up to the cabin. I dumped it about a hundred yards back when I heard your shot. If the eggs are broken, it's all your fault."

Wasn't it *always* her fault, Leslie asked herself. She knew better than to give into her impulses. She wasn't a spontaneous person. Her life was much less stressful when she kept it simple and logical. As for Joe Bonner and his trickery, well, she'd have to find another way to deal with him.

Trying to make amends for her misdeed, Leslie volunteered to cook the scrambled eggs for their brunch. When Joe asked if she could cook eggs better than she made coffee, which she'd forgotten and left to boil over, she assured him she could. However, there was no omelette pan or cheese grater, no electric toaster or juice maker. Under such primitive conditions she was forced to tax her ingenuity.

"This is good," Joe said, bobbing his head in approval over what Leslie had dubbed "eggs hors concours." "I usually don't eat this fancy stuff. It's a nice change. What are these green things?"

"Don't you know?" she asked, growing worried that she had committed yet another error. She had returned to the near empty garden, hoping for inspiration when her meal began to look as plain as eggs. A clump of chives and some of the vegetables Joe had bought were a help. She'd tasted one of the chives to be sure of what they were, but if Joe didn't recognize his own produce . . .

"Where'd it come from?"

"Your garden."

"My garden?" He was starting to look seriously concerned.

"Didn't you say that was a garden at the side of the house?"

"Well, yes, but there isn't anything planted in it yet. I haven't had the time."

The longer he looked at her as if she might have poisoned him, the more resentful she became. She wasn't totally stupid. She'd gone to college. She held down a good job. She could cook up a storm in a civilized kitchen. And she knew a chive when she saw one. "Well, you got yourself a great little crop of chives out there now, Mr. Bonner. Believe you me," she told him as she slapped her hand down on the table and looked him straight in the eye, daring him to argue with her.

Joe laughed. "Good. Terrific," he said dryly, chuckling quietly and giving her a wary eye. "They taste great in eggs."

Maybe she had overreacted a little, she thought, as Joe went silently back to eating his eggs. But she was tired of feeling like a total incompetent around this man. Everyone who knew her thought she was always in control, always organized, and always up on everything. She wanted Joe to think so too.

After their meal, Joe went straight to work. Leslie did the dishes and quickly ran out of things to do. She'd already been out of doors once that day, and she'd admired the view while she was there. So unless there was a good reason to go out again, she'd just as soon stay inside where she belonged. Of course, Joe was a neat, clean person, so there wasn't much to do in the cabin either. She didn't own anything in the vicinity but a purse and a cut up dress. She went to her purse in search of entertainment.

While Joe plunked away at his little computer, Leslie cleaned out her wallet and put her credit cards in alphabetical order. She checked the shade of her lipstick and decided to save it for when the rescue party came. She counted the keys on her key ring and took the time to wonder why Joe had bothered to take them out of the ignition, since neither she nor her car were going anywhere. At last she found a distraction—a silver nail file tucked away at the bottom of her bag.

With great verve she set about her manicure. On the third nail, she looked up to find Joe staring at her. A scowl of displeasure looking very at home on his face.

"What?" she asked innocently.

"Must you do that?"

"What? My nails?"

"It's very distracting."

That was exactly why she was doing them, but she got his point just the same. "Sorry."

Joe went back to work, and Leslie tiptoed over to the kitchen sink for a glass of water. There was an old-fashioned hand pump that needed to be primed a little before water came out of it, but he hadn't seemed to mind the noise when she'd been doing the dishes. Joe's plunking slowed down but didn't stop while she got her drink.

She recalled seeing some saltine crackers in one of the cupboards and quietly sought them out. She opened the crackling cellophane wrapper and removed several, because the eggs hadn't satisfied her appetite. Not a big eater normally, and never a snacker, Leslie chalked this lapse in her behavior up to the mountain air. Everyone knew it made you hungrier than usual.

"Is that going to take long?" Joe's exasperation was a surprise to Leslie. Now what had she done?

"What?"

"All the wrapper rustling and cracker crunching," he said, annoyed.

"Excuse me. I'm sorry," she said, walking back to the couch, flopping herself down despondently. "I'll just sit right here, and I won't make a sound. I promise."

"Look. I'm sorry. But I have to get this done. I'm not used to having someone around while I work. I told you I wasn't easy to live with."

"So, work. I'll be very quiet. You won't even know I'm here."

Joe's expression was dubious, but he seemed willing to give it another try. She sat like a statue of *The Thinker* for awhile, then leaned back into the couch and got comfortable. She tried to remember some of her favorite music and played it back in her head. But when her moccasin-shod feet began to tap lightly on the floor, she had to stop. She closed her eyes, thinking she'd try to find her alpha level through meditation. It was something she'd always thought interesting but never had the time to try. After several minutes of trying to relax, she found herself listening to Joe's plunking. It was terribly disturbing. She sighed and gave up on her alpha waves. But she didn't reopen her eyes.

Joe. Joe Bonner. She liked his name. It was a very plain name for an extraordinary man. Her mind crawled back to the morning hours when he'd so rudely touched her when he discovered she wasn't really hurt. For all his anger, his hands had been remarkably gentle. What would his touch be like if he weren't angry? What if he were feeling amorous and favorably inclined toward her? Her body sighed from head to toe at the thought. What if he were even more gentle? What if his strokes were intended to arouse her, to drive her wild with desire? What if he'd started to undress her, looking for her wound? What if he'd touched her bare skin, caressed her naked breasts until they were on fire with insatiable yearning? What if . . . ?

"For crying out loud, Leslie! What the hell are you doing over there? Having an orgasm?"

Her eyes popped open. "Who me?"

Joe was turning to face her as she swung her feet to the floor and sat up. "Sigh, sigh, groan. You could do sound tracks for porno movies. What are you doing?"

"Nothing. I was trying to be quiet. But excuse me for breathing, Mr. Bonner. I'll try to do better in the future," she said defensively, so he wouldn't see the guilt she was feeling.

"This isn't going to work," he said, "But, I have an idea."

"What?" she muttered under her breath, still feeling foolish about her daydreams, still feeling the effect they had on her body.

Joe walked to the door and looked back at her when she didn't follow. "Out here."

"Oh, great," she mumbled, rolling off the couch and getting to her feet to shuffle along behind him. Out the door and around the side of the cabin she followed him, until he stopped at his would-be garden.

"You seem to know your chives. How would you like to plant some more conventional veggies like carrots and potatoes and lettuce? If I can get back to my truck before too long, you can plant tomatoes too. I bought some plants, but they may die before I get back to them."

Hands on her hips, Leslie looked first at the plot of dirt, then at Joe. "Are you joking?"

"No. It'll give you something to do. Something to be proud of. And I won't have to be yelling at you constantly to be quiet." He grinned. "It'll be good for our morale."

"If I say no, are you going to force me to do this?"

A strange look crossed Joe's face, and again he grinned—this time it wasn't with humor. He took several steps toward her. He was several inches taller than she, and she had to force her head back so she could keep eye contact with him. His green gaze bore into her, searching deeply for secret treasures he was greedy to possess. She took a step backward and then another. Joe continued to advance on her until her back was against the rough wood of the cabin. When his arms moved up on either side of her to block her escape, she didn't flinch or break contact with the keen stare that was more her captor than his physical form was.

For long minutes he stood there, close but not touching her, wondering but not asking. "Funny, that you should mention force. I can't recall one time when I've actually forced you to do something you didn't want to do," he finally said in a low, menacing voice. "Why would you bring up something like that unless you'd been thinking about it? Have you been thinking of my forcing you to do something you don't want to do, Les? Is that why you brought it up? Do you *want* me to force you to do something you don't want to do? Does that excite you?" he asked, aligning his zipper to hers and leaning into it firmly.

There had to be anger in her somewhere, she thought, frantically searching for it. He had no right to treat her like this. Her pulse was racing so fast and her breathing was so shallow, she couldn't sort out her emotions. Even her sensory system was on the blink. Instead of repulsion, she felt like one raw, totally exposed nerve ending. She was frightened and excited. She wanted to run away and melt into his arms at the same time. The turmoil seized her vocal cords, and she didn't deny him.

He lowered his head. His lips touched the soft, sensitive skin just below her right ear and moved slowly across her throat as he rubbed his body against hers, pressing against her breasts until he could reach her other ear, her temple, her forehead, the corner of her mouth. His mouth closed over hers, his tongue stroking, demanding entrance.

He pulled back. "Is this part of the game? Am I supposed to force my way in? Is that what makes you hot?" he asked, his voice harsh with his own need, which already was evident as it pressed urgently into her belly.

Unbeckoned and from out of nowhere, tears clouded her eyes. She wanted him to continue; she wanted to open up to him, but not just physically. Tiny drops rolled down her cheeks. Joe saw them and hesitated briefly, astutely, before he lapped them up with his tongue and went back to her lips. This time, however, he wasn't overbearing.

He removed his hand from the wall behind her and cupped her face tenderly. He placed a chaste kiss to her lips, then sealed it there, ever so gently, with the pad of his thumb. "Leslie. I wouldn't ever force you to do anything you didn't want to do. Nothing. I want you. I guess that's becoming obvious, isn't it? But not by force." He paused. "The garden is there to keep you busy. But not by force. Never by force."

They stood there for several more moments, both refusing to release the energy they had created. Joe removed the remaining few tears on Leslie's face with a soft stroke of the back of his hand. "You okay?" She nodded numbly. "I'm not going to apologize for this either. I enjoyed it too much. And you don't have to work in the garden. But I'm asking you to please stay outside for a while, so I can get some work done. Okay?"

She nodded once more and sucked in a huge breath as he moved away from her. He glanced back at her once before rounding the corner of the cabin. His look had been filled with mixed emotions, and she knew he was feeling the same turbulence inside that she felt.

She hadn't flexed a muscle since he'd pinned her to the wall. Long after he left her, she remained rooted to the same spot, too weak to do anything more than breathe in and out. She tried to decipher the meaning of her response to Joe's assault on her senses, but her mind was a blank, an unearthly, rapturous void of nothingness for the first time in her life. It was as if Joe Bonner had the power to kiss away her ability to reason, to judge, and to make choices. Curiously she didn't perceive this as an altogether bad thing. She found she liked it. Being totally sensorial was a new experience she wouldn't mind repeating. But if a next time came, she wanted Joe to know what he was doing to her. She wanted him to come to her with gentleness in his heart; tenderly, the way he had the first night when he'd listened to her talk; with consideration, the way he had when he'd tended to her blisters; with real emotions, the way he had when he thought she was hurt. Not with anger.

Next time. The idea appealed to her. She tried to remember the last time she wanted a man as much as she wanted Joe and found that it never existed. Her body had ached for the closeness only a man could supply, late in the night, alone in the darkness. But no man had ever awakened images in her mind of the two of them together, their bodies entwined and throbbing with passion. Joe did. Joe brought to life so many things in her that she never knew were there: Desire and excitement, need and a wish to please, anger, frustration, and shame.

Leslie released a slow breath. Joe made her feel, that was for sure. It seemed odd that she could almost hate him and want to know him better in the same second, but she did.

Inside the cabin, Joe began to plunk away at the computer keys again, slowly and with a lot of back-spacing. His concentration was poor, and every other word was showing up misspelled. It didn't matter if Leslie was in the cabin or not, she was on his mind, jamming his brain waves.

Every time he turned around, everywhere he looked, there she was with those deep blue eyes sparkling with humor or anger or curiosity. He could feel her all around him, warm and yielding. He was having a hell of a time keeping his hands off her. His resolve not to get involved with her was wearing thin. He couldn't remember wanting a woman more. But Les-lie Rothe?

He hadn't fully recovered from her little stunt ear-lier in the day. The panic he'd felt at seeing her lying there in the dirt, motionless, came back too fresh and too easily. And moments ago outside, watching her raven black hair blowing in the wind, her chin set rebelliously, her stance become defiant, he couldn't seem to control himself. There was something in him that wanted to tame and possess her. He wanted to teach her to love, to give and accept love with her body. He wanted her to trust him. He wanted to hear his name on her lips. Joe. Joe. Joe.

The trouble was, did he want it because she was a beautiful woman who had not the slightest interest in him? Or was he truly attracted to Leslie? Did he want her to want him because she'd never loved someone before? Or because he needed her to love him? She was a worldly woman with an innocent heart, and he, maybe better than most people, knew how fragile a heart was. If he set out to win her heart, he should damn well want to keep it. That would only be fair.

Determinedly, he turned back to his work. He'd give this thing with Leslie a little more time to see if his first instincts were right. Then, before he got carried away for all the wrong reasons, he'd arrange for an early rescue.

A few hours later, a grubby, dirty Leslie leaned her hoe against the outside wall of the cabin and tried in vain to brush the part of the garden she was wearing back down where it belonged. With a critical eye, she surveyed her efforts. For someone who grew her own herbs in lovely coordinated pots on her kitchen windowsill, she hadn't done such a bad job on this much less chic way of farming. In fact, she almost wished she'd be there when it finally came up from the ground and became fruitful . . . or in this case vegetableful. She'd love to see the expression on Joe's face when he found he was the owner of an anomalous garden.

The idea had occurred to her shortly after the giddiness caused by Joe's kiss had worn off. It was the perfect way to pay him back for every mean and cruel thing he'd done since they met. As a bonus to the idea, it was also something she could cherish in her heart and laugh about the next time he was nasty to her—and there wasn't a doubt in her mind about there being a next time for that.

She'd spent most of the afternoon hoeing wonderfully straight and even furrows in the loose soil so as not to arouse his suspicions. The next day, she would begin her creative seed planting. Although, if he were especially kind and friendly toward her later, she always could change her plan.

With the light and airy step of a person about to wreak revenge on the enemy, Leslie all but skipped up to the cabin door. She listened at the door to hear if Joe was still working. There was no sound, but then computers didn't make much noise. Prudently, she knocked on the door. When there was no answer, she repeated the gesture with more force.

A sleepy-eyed Joe answered her summons.

"Can I come in now? Or should I wait till you finish your nap?" she asked, irked that he'd been sleeping while she'd been outside breaking her back over his garden.

"Give me a break," he muttered, still drowsy. "I'm not a rock. I haven't been able to sleep as well as you have the past couple of nights."

"Oh, sure. Blame that on me too." Stepping past him into the cabin, she caught a look in his eyes that actually did indicate he accused her of being the cause. She ignored it as a luscious aroma reached her nose and made her salivate. "You cooked dinner," she said, amazed.

"Well, what do you think I did before you came along? Call for Chinese takeout?"

"No. But I guess I assumed . . ." She let her words trail off, realizing she had misjudged him again.

"You assumed you'd have to do all the cooking because you're a woman," he finished for her. "That would have been very unliberated of me to presume such a thing, now, wouldn't it?"

Leslie smiled at him. "Yes, it would have been." She was impressed that he hadn't. It wasn't exactly in keeping with the character traits he'd presented to her so far. "Do I have time to wash up and change clothes?"

"Yes. And am I to assume that's my signal to take a hike?"

Again, she smiled, appreciating that he hadn't made one of his usual lurid comments. She got the distinct impression he was trying to be nice to her, to get along with her. Perhaps he was making amends for his earlier behavior, or maybe he was trying to bridge the gap that had formed between them when they'd swung their cars off the road. Whatever his reasons, Leslie was grateful. She didn't want to fight with him anymore. She wanted to know him better.

Seven

Leslie's sink bath and Joe's dinner went uninterrupted by strife. Joe had prepared venison, which Leslie wasn't at all sure she was going to like. But not wanting to offend him again, she tasted it and found it not too bad. She thought she might even grow to like it.

A fire snapped and glowed in the fireplace, and kerosene lamps were lit. Aside from the little gasoline generator that ran only three hours a night in order to keep the battery-operated refrigerator charged, there was no electricity. Even Joe's computer ran on batteries, but he seemed to have an ample supply of those. Leslie found it extremely inconvenient that nothing was instant or laborless, but there wasn't anything she could do about it. She simply added it to the reasons why she preferred to stay in the city; although, she had to admit, the firelight made things very cozy and romantic.

Mountain nights, however, proved to be just as boring as mountain days. There were no reports for her to review, no places to go with her friends, nothing to see or watch or listen to.

"What are you working on?" she asked Joe in a quiet voice, desperate for conversation.

"Can we talk about this later? I'm on a roll here."

"Sure. Sorry." With that avenue closed to her, she had nothing left to do but think. And invariably, her thoughts turned to questions. It was her nature to question. "What happens when we run out of food? I mean, even after you've gone back for the food in your truck?"

"I'll kill something, and we'll have berries for dessert," Joe said absently without looking up from his writing.

"It's much colder here in the winter. Will we be warm enough? With just this fire? You don't usually stay all winter, do you?"

"I go back to Denver in the fall. And we'll be rescued before then. Don't worry." He leaned over to see what he'd typed, corrected an error, and continued.

"But what if my family can't find the cars. The mountains are the last place . . . Well, they won't even bother looking in the mountains, because it's not someplace I'd normally go." She felt like a fool for not having thought of this before. She should have been more worried all along. "We're going to die up here."

The plunking stopped, and Joe turned to face her with a droll expression. "I have a family too. And friends. And a mortgage to pay. If I don't show up eventually, somebody is bound to come looking. Better yet, I have an agent that's half bloodhound. When I don't meet my deadline because of your incessant chattering, he'll come after us. But that won't exactly be a joyous occasion, if you get my drift."

"I'm sorry," she said, downcast. "I'm bored."

"What you need is a really good book to read," he said enthusiastically. He stood and plucked a book from one of the shelves overhead, then turned back to Leslie with a smug look on his face. "This one just happens to be one of my favorites."

The book he'd chosen for her was oversize and almost two inches thick. On the glossy cover was a picture similar to other pictures she'd seen in magazines and newspapers. A large-eyed, frail-boned, emaciated child stared back at her pathetically. Joe had written a book on the African famine. And he'd been right, again. If this was a sample of his writing, it was involved and more than Leslie cared to take on as light reading. Not that she was totally without feeling. She made her share of charitable contributions every year. It made her feel good, and it looked good on her tax forms. But she'd had no real interest in following up on what good her money was doing. Other people made their own careers fighting for causes, her career was in front of a computer.

"You wrote this?" she asked. Joe didn't seem the type to get involved in human causes. Hiding himself away in the mountains didn't exactly denote an interest in society.

"Yep. These too." He passed her several more volumes. All were beautifully covered and impressive, but they were all on subjects such as arms control, vanishing species, and nuclear waste. All were, in Leslie's opinion, terribly depressing. "Take your pick. They're all great reading," Joe boasted.

Feeling as if she were being pushed from behind and hating to disappoint or insult Joe, who obviously was proud of his work, she took the book on vanishing species and laid the others aside. Who knew, there might be some valuable information in it she could use, like bears spend their summer vacations in Alaska and cougars are really vegetarians.

The first chapter had vivid pictures and a graphic description of the plight of baby seals. Her stomach rolled at the sight of the sad-eyed pups, beaten and bloodied for their pelts. Joe addressed other problems dealing with animals that were disappearing by the hundreds of thousands every year and not being allowed to reproduce. He went into great detail on some that were nearly extinct, including the American bald eagle, and what measures were being taken to save them. He was an excellent writer. He undertook the issue with a great deal of common sense and compassion, and left, at least his newest reader, deeply moved and outraged.

She wasn't halfway through the book before she felt the overwhelming urge to cry again. Not for the animals she was reading about but for herself. Where had she been for so long? She was aware, vaguely, that there were endangered animals, but she'd always thought of it as someone else's problem, someone else's job to take care of them. Consequently, she hadn't cared what was happening. It didn't involve her directly, so why should she? But she should have, because it did.

What if the people managing these animals were as stupid and unfeeling as she had been with the mountain? What if they allowed the birds and animals to disappear off the face of the earth never to exist again? Just as she had allowed, even encouraged, the destruction of an entire mountain that never could be replaced, for the sake of her job, for money. What then?

Heartsick she flipped the book closed and looked over at Joe, seeing him in a whole new light. He might be obnoxious and pompous sometimes, but she had to credit him with a lot more integrity and conscience than she had. He finished the sentence he was working on, tacking on the period with great flare, then he turned to her.

"Finished already?" he asked, leaning back in his chair as if he had nothing to do. He plainly was waiting for her opinion of the book, and she had no idea of what to say.

How could she tell him that she couldn't carry on a decent conversation on any of the subjects he'd written about because she knew nothing about them? Because she'd never taken the time to learn. Because she hadn't cared. How could she tell this man, who seemed so interested in the world he lived in, that she wasn't? That she'd lived in her own orbit for so long she had no idea of what was going on outside its limited range. She was filled with self-disgust and scorn and too ashamed to admit the truth.

"It's very interesting," she said truthfully, unsure of anything else she honestly could add. "It must be hard to stay objective and write with so much feeling."

"I'm not objective. I wouldn't have chosen those subjects to write about if I were." That made sense, too, so Leslie nodded. "I care very much, and writing about them is the only way I could think of to help. It isn't enough, but it's all I know."

There was a dense silence in the cabin. Leslie was at a loss for words. She wouldn't lie to him by agreeing with everything he said. And she didn't know enough to ask questions—yet. But very soon, she would. She'd make sure of it. She didn't want to feel this ignorant or insensitive ever again. No wonder her mother thought she had no feelings. When had Leslie ever given evidence that she did?

"You were right, though. It's very involved reading," she told Joe, not able to look him directly in the eye. "Do you happen to have anything a bit lighter?"

A flash of something . . . disappointment, maybe, crossed Joe's features, but he didn't speak his thoughts. Instead he stood and went to another set of shelves where three or four dozen paperback books were lined neatly in a row. "These don't usually appeal to women, but other than reference books, they're all I've got."

Leslie took the book he held out to her and turned it over in her hands. It was a Max Darkwood novel. She was very familiar with the author's name. He was her father's favorite. For more years than she could remember, her father had passed his leisure hours with his nose stuck in a Max Darkwood western. Leslie's taste leaned toward biographies, family sagas, or travel books, but if this was her alternative . . .

While Joe went back to his latest project, Leslie dove into the world of Max Darkwood. Written in the first person, with the hero never addressed as anything but "stranger," the reader soon sensed that the writer and the hero were, indeed, one and the same. He was a no-nonsense kind of hombre with a cold stare and a deadly six shooter. He wasn't lookin' for no trouble, but he didn't take any guff off nobody neither. His dog's name was Spit and both were deadly to have as enemies.

In this particular story, an evil rancher was driving homesteaders off their land. The railroad was on its way through, and land values were going up. There was a farmer's daughter with real spirit who kept imperiling herself with the evil rancher. She was really a very foolish girl, to Leslie's way of thinking. She should have let the men handle the rancher. The girl was constantly making a mess of things and having to be rescued by Max. At one point she was caught in a cave, alone with the rancher. He was advancing, intending to do her bodily harm. Her heart was racing like a locomotive. . . .

"I'm going to bed."

Leslie looked up from her reclining position on the couch to find Joe standing above her, his arms full of bed linens. "Oh. Already? What time is it?"

"After ten," he said, frowning as he watched her. "You didn't have any trouble getting into Max Darkwood. Do you like him?"

"More than I thought I would." She got to her fee
and took the linens and blankets from Joe. "I migh
read a little longer, if it's okay." Joe was being so
quiet and guarded with his thoughts, she wasn'
sure of his mood.

"Turn the lamp off before you go to sleep. Good
night."

His impersonal words, softly spoken though they
were, seemed a rather abrupt and unsatisfactory
ending to a day neither one of them was likely to
forget. There were words that needed to be spoken
but they were both reluctant to say them. Instead
they chose to suffer through an awkward moment o
cowardice.

"Good night," Leslie finally answered, refusing to
break eye contact with him for a long time.

"Enjoy your story," Joe said, even though the ex
pression on his face was saying something quite
different. Then he turned and went to the side o
the bed.

She sat on the couch, meticulously keeping he
eyes averted, all the while listening attentively to the
muffled noises coming from across the room. There
was the distinctive ping of Joe's belt buckle hitting
the floor and the rustle of sheets being drawn back
and the squeak of the bed springs as Joe laid hi
weight upon it. And then there was silence, except
in Leslie's mind. Over and over again it replayed th
feel of Joe's hands on her body, his kiss, the pres
sure of his body against hers, and the gentleness
with which he'd dried her tears.

A quick glance at the quilt covered lump in th
bed reminded her that Joe had made no further
overtures toward her sincerely or in jest. He'd sai
he wanted her, but maybe his was a purely take-i
or-leave-it attitude. Perhaps he wasn't having th
difficulty with his emotions that she was. He migh

not want to get to know her any better than he already did. He probably knew more about her by now than he ever really wanted to. And he most likely wasn't crazy about any of it.

With a despondent sigh through pursed lips, feeling alone and lonely, she picked up the Max Darkwood novel. The evil rancher ripped the farm girl's bodice away from her body and was about to commit the vilest of all acts upon her, when suddenly, from out of nowhere, Max was there to slit the rancher's throat with his jagged-edged hunting knife. The farm girl was upset, but Max calmed her with soft words and gentle kisses.

They left the cave. Max wrapped the girl in his blanket and they began the long journey home. But before they got there, the girl's beauty overwhelmed poor Max, and she was so grateful for his assistance that she threw herself at him. Max was forced to make wild, passionate, explicit love to her there on the desert floor under the grinning moon. In the last chapter, Max tipped his hat at the girl when he left her at her father's farm. Then he rode off to Yuma in search of his son, the boy borne by the beautiful Indian princess Glowing Moon some eight years earlier.

Late to bed and early to rise didn't agree well with Leslie. She even had to forfeit her dozing time, as Joe was already at his computer when she woke up.

He couldn't have missed the sounds of her getting up and sitting with her feet on the floor and her head in her hands, but he apparently chose to ignore them. She stretched and yawned dramatically, trying to get his attention. The least he could do was say good morning, before he blocked her out of his world.

Giving up, she felt not the slightest need to be modest as she walked to the chest of drawers for a towel and clean clothes, wearing nothing but Joe's pajama top. It covered all the basics—just barely—and Joe wasn't likely to notice anyway.

Gratifyingly, as she walked into Joe's field of vision, the computer keys slowed to a stop, and she smiled slyly. She wanted to turn and see the expression on his face but didn't want to appear too interested. So she added a little extra sway to her walk and moved on to the dresser. She could catch his expression on her way back across the room.

She never considered herself a person with an overabundance of feminine wiles, but she sure had a bad case of them now. She ran her fingers through her hair in a very absent manner to detangle and fluff it up a little. She was careful to hold her clean laundry in one hand rather than up close to her body. She wanted to make sure Joe saw all there was to see, and she wanted it to hold his attention.

The typing had started again, but the rhythm was erratic and he didn't seem to have his usual light touch. His fingers came to a slow, faltering stop when she turned to face him. She saw his lips part and watched his throat muscles move as he took a hard swallow. Her temperature rose by several degrees as his ravaging gaze slipped over her body from top to toe and back again. She was more than satisfied with his reaction.

"Good morning. You're starting early today," she said, pretending not to notice that he was staring at her rudely. His gaze dropped to her chest, and she felt her breasts swell and harden. There was a slight nod of his head as he agreed with her statement . . . or was he agreeing with what he saw? Either way, Leslie was enjoying being in the center of his limelight and wanted to prolong it. "Don't let me disturb you. I'd like a bath, but I can wait till you're at a good place to stop."

She moseyed over to the stove and took her time pouring herself a cup of coffee. She sat down at the table and crossed her legs, knowing that the night shirt was covering much less of her at this point. "Do you happen to remember which Max Darkwood novel told the story about the Indian princess Glowing Moon?" she asked casually.

Again Joe simply nodded his head and, moving like a zombie, got up to retrieve it from the shelf. When she rose and stepped forward to take it from his outstretched hand, she was startled when his other hand grabbed her by the wrist. She looked up into his intense and perceptive eyes and suddenly felt she was in great danger. But she wasn't afraid. She welcomed the sensation of fear, beckoned to it without flinching. When Joe spoke, his voice was thick and deeper than usual. "Watch your step, Leslie. I'm not a patient man. Nor am I a virtuous one. I suggest you think twice before you start playing games you know nothing about."

With a brazenness she never dreamed she had, she smiled at him, heedlessly shook loose of his grip and stood defiantly before him. In that moment it was as if she'd found the magic key that fit the beautiful box that was handed down by every grandmother to mother to daughter. She'd been in possession of the box since birth. Always there but never opened, Leslie had paid little attention to it—until now.

Gem encrusted, it was the contents of the box that held the real value. For within lay all the precious secrets women had used for generations to attract, ensnare, and eventually capture the men they wanted. She *did* know the rules to the games men and women played. And much, much more. All along she'd known. They were as innately part of her as her ability to be logical and organized. She simply had never chosen to play the games Joe was talking about before. And why did she want so badly to play now? The answer to that was simple and logical. She'd never wanted anyone before now, never wanted anyone before Joe Bonner.

Joe's eyes narrowed, and he studied her cautiously and with great trepidation. He sensed a difference in her and wasn't sure of what to do. But not being patient and having no virtues didn't mean he wasn't prudent. He went outside to get the bathtub for Leslie.

The noonday sun was hot. Leslie had removed the flannel shirt hours ago, and still she could feel beads of perspiration rolling down between her breasts. The T-shirt clung to her damp skin, and strands of hair matted themselves to the sides of her face. Artistic farming was hard work. She couldn't help but wonder if it might not have been easier just to do it the conventional way. She shook her head. The expression on Joe's face when he discovered what she'd done would be worth all the work, even if she wasn't there to see it. She'd have wonderful dreams about it though.

She'd planted two rows of carrots diagonally from corner to corner to form an X. Radishes would form a circle around the X. Lettuce patches were placed at each loose end of the X, and there would be cucumber and squash vines coming up where he least expected them. The peas were a problem she planned to save for later.

She sat on the ground and wiped her forehead with the back of her arm while she surveyed her efforts. She'd rather sleep with a bear than admit it to anyone, but she'd enjoyed the morning tremendously. Not because of what she done to Joe's garden, but because there was something real about the dirt under her nails and the healthy ache in her back. The birds had sung to her all morning, and sometimes a gentle breeze brought to her one of the sweetest odors she'd ever smelled, a scent finer than any perfume she was familiar with. She hadn't the slightest intention of becoming an outdoor person, but she had enjoyed the change of pace.

"Looks as if you've done quite a bit out here." Joe's voice made Leslie jump, and she turned to find him lounging against the corner of the cabin. "Ready for lunch?"

"Yes. I'm starving," she said, her heart lurching at the sight of him. She stood to dust the soil off her jeans and follow him in. But after taking a few steps, she saw that he wasn't moving. His eyes were focused on her clinging T-shirt. She was only too aware that the tips of her breasts were hard and pressed tightly against the damp cotton material. Her first instinct was to cover herself, but she boldly refused to do so.

All night long she'd dreamed of Joe. The tender, gentle Joe she knew he could be. He'd held her, touched her, kissed her. He'd taken her to Eden and had brought her back safe and contented. She wanted him, and she wasn't above flaunting herself to get him. She was obsessed with the idea of Joe being a soft, considerate lover. She wanted Joe to be her lover. No, she hesitated briefly, it was more than that. She wanted Joe to love her, to teach her what love felt like, and she longed to share with him the secrets of the box.

It made sense to Leslie. After all, Joe had already made her feel so many emotions she normally refused to acknowledge, why couldn't he make her feel love as well?

Again she had to strain her imagination to pretend that she didn't know what Joe was doing or thinking. She bent over to pick up her discarded shirt and continued to amble toward the cabin. She almost fell over when his voice boomed out in anger, echoing through the trees. "Where the hell did you get that? And who the hell gave you permission to use it?"

"What?" This time Leslie truly was scared. Joe wasn't just testy or mocking in his ire. He was outraged.

"That tie. My tie. My lucky tie," he wailed, his fist clenching and unclenching in frustration.

"This tie?" she asked, looking down to where Joe's furious gaze was riveted, at the tie she was using for a belt. "I picked the ugliest one of the bunch. You honestly don't wear it, do you?"

Joe stared at her in shock. That he wanted to punch her was a little too apparent for Leslie. She knew he wouldn't, but then, Joe had his own ways of getting his revenge. Suddenly he tilted his head back and released an unholy howl of defeat. "Are you *trying* to drive me crazy? Because if you are, you're succeeding."

In the time it took her to blink, Leslie was in his arms. He took a fist full of her hair and pulled her head back so he could look down at her face. His breath was warm and minty as it mingled with hers. His green gaze seemed to invade her mind, seek out her soul, question the essence of her being. His voice was a grating whisper. "My body burns for you. You've driven my mind to total distraction. And now you've destroyed my lucky tie. What else do you want from me, Leslie? What will you take from me next?"

In the most natural act of her life, Leslie rose up on tiptoe and pressed her lips to Joe's in a light, sweet kiss. When he frowned and seemed to be confused, she did it again. When she looked for his reaction, his eyes narrowed with comprehension and skepticism. There was pain, wonder, several questions, and finally regret in his eyes. "You're tempting, and Lord knows you'd be easy pickings, sweet Leslie. I'm just not sure I should be the one to do it."

There was a jolt, as Leslie's feet hit the ground when he released her and walked away from her toward the woods. She wanted to call out to him, but what would she say? He didn't want her. It hadn't even crossed her mind that if she offered herself, he might refuse. Her ego was dashed to smithereens. Worse, though, was the hollow, empty feeling that settled in her chest and began to unfold and grow disproportionately, until it made breathing difficult and brought tears to her eyes. As if she were dragging her heart behind her, she walked dejectedly into the cabin to see if she could get the wrinkles out of Joe's lucky tie.

For the next few days, the tension in the little cabin was so thick and heavy, they could have cut it with a knife. Joe spent most of his time trying to meet his deadline. His answers to what few questions Leslie could bring herself to ask were monosyllabic. They were too polite to each other, too wary, too cautious in their attempts to avoid any further confrontations.

Leslie's days took on an orderly routine, which suited her just fine. She kept a pair of jeans beside the couch and was always careful to be completely covered when she moved around the cabin. She went straight to the garden after breakfast to work there, which after she'd finished planting, consisted of filling buckets of water at the outside pump and pouring them on the garden. That done, the rest of the day was hers.

Still too ashamed to let Joe know or give him a chance to suspect that she virtually knew nothing of the issues he cared so much about, she had taken to smuggling his books out of the cabin in her clothes with a Max Darkwood as a decoy. She sat behind the woodshed, where she'd be able to see Joe approaching if he ever gave in to a whim to check on her. And she read every word with the thirst of a born-again Christian rereading the Bible. At night in the cabin, she read only Max Darkwood novels. And when the lamps went out and all was quiet, Max came to her in her dreams. Where Joe couldn't bring himself to care, Max did. He listened to her irrational thoughts, understood her, and was patient with her selfishness and ignorance. Max was tender and soothing. He was dangerous and exciting and gentle enough to accept Leslie and her love.

Eight

"I'm going back down to the truck this morning. Is there anything in the trunk of your car that you want?" Joe asked nearly a week after the fatal Saturday they'd run each other off the road.

"No, thanks." Leslie said, her nose nestled up against a Max Darkwood novel. In it a preacher's daughter was posing as a saloon girl while she gathered information against the nefarious town marshal who shot her father and brother down in cold blood—right in front of the church, no less.

"I'll be gone most of the day. So stay close to the cabin. If it gets too dark, I'll have to make camp."

"Okay." Max was just about to intercept a would-be customer of the so-called saloon girl's who was drunk and—

"If I never come back, there's a pot of gold buried under this cabin, and you can have it," Joe said, his tone huffy.

She looked up at him then, bewildered by his sudden affront. "Now what have I done?" she asked, feeling sure he had nothing to complain about. She rubbed her moccasin-covered feet together absently. Her feet were almost completely healed, but the skin itched like crazy.

"You haven't done anything. That's the whole point. You haven't done anything but read those damn books for days."

"I work in your damned garden every day. I do my share of housework," she said, letting his anger feed hers. "What else would you like me to do? Chop the wood? Polish your boots?"

"No. That's not what I meant. I don't have any complaints about your helping out around here. I just . . . I was just . . . well, how come you haven't read any of my books?"

"I will. I'll be here a while. I like the Max Darkwood stories, but I'm bound to run out of them sooner or later."

"Oh. So then you'll read mine. As a last resort against total boredom."

Leslie groaned as she realized she had, once again, stuck her foot in it. "No. I didn't mean to say it that way. I'll read one today. They're very good books. I—"

"Don't bother," Joe broke in on her explanation. "You know why you prefer those stupid novels to my books? Because mine tell about the real world, Leslie." His voice grew bitter and incensed. His features were full of disappointment. "You're uncomfortable reading about what's real, because you're afraid you'll have to wake up and face it someday. And then, oh, heaven forbid, you might have to feel something. But you don't want to do that because you're too wrapped up in yourself to give a damn about anything else. That's exactly why you've never fallen in love. Because you can't see anything or anyone two feet in front of you. And that's exactly why you'll wind up spending the rest of your life alone."

Too stunned to speak, she watched as Joe stomped out of the cabin, slamming the door behind him. It was several seconds before she could remember to draw air into her lungs. Her heart felt sluggish, as if it wanted to stop. She stared thoughtlessly at the door, too shocked to know how deeply hurt she was. The pain, however, refused to go unnoticed. Slowly it began to gnaw at her from the inside out. It tore and split and wrenched at her life center, until it ruptured and broke.

Joe covered half the distance back to his truck before he ran out of steam. It became slowly but clearly evident to him that he wasn't nearly as angry with Leslie as he was with himself. She was a beautiful, intelligent woman. So what if she wasn't politically active? Lots of people weren't and that didn't make them human waste. No, his problem with Leslie was purely personal and something he had to work out on his own.

The trouble was, he wanted her. He'd been falling head over heels in love with her from the moment he set eyes on her. She had courage and fortitude and could be as tough as nails when she had to be. How often had he come awake in the night wishing she was in his arms? How many hours had he sat watching her sleep with only the dawn to light her soft, sweet features? When had she invaded his mind so completely that he couldn't work, couldn't sleep, couldn't have a private thought without her presence in it? He hung on her every word, memorized her movements and expressions. He felt driven to know all there was to know about her. Who she was, what she thought, how she arrived at a specific conclusion. More than anything, he needed to possess her heart. He craved her concern, her love, her friendship. His desire was to fill her with a passion so great, so real and vivid that she couldn't live without him. When she'd offered herself to him, had she known what he wanted from her? Was she capable of that kind of love?

The last time he'd asked so much from a woman she'd failed him. Or maybe he'd failed her first somehow. All he knew was that for months he'd lived with his head in the clouds, madly in love, thinking he'd discovered paradise. Their love was perfect, romantic and filled with passion and laughter. Perfect, he'd thought, until he discovered that she'd been seeing other men all that time and then refused to give them up.

Leslie didn't even know what love was. What if she found it so wonderful that she'd need more than he could give her? What if his life and heart and soul weren't enough for her either? Did he want to take that kind of risk again?

On the other hand, women were no more alike than men were. What if he and Leslie had been destined for each other all along? What if he was making a horrible mistake in not letting Leslie into his life? What if he was making an even bigger mistake in not opening her life up to the world, to him in particular? What if her heart was an untapped source of endless, ever-flowing love? How could he possibly ignore it or turn away from it in cowardice?

By the time Joe reached his truck, it was early afternoon. He'd had six hours to call himself everything from an abject fool to a yellow-bellied idiot. It was time to get over his fears and take another stab at happiness. He couldn't spend the rest of his life cowering in corners and loving from afar. In the next six hours, the time it would take him to get back to Leslie, he'd bolster his courage and try to figure out how he'd get her to forgive him.

Darkness had settled in for the night by the time Joe reached the turnoff from the main logging road to the access road leading to the cabin. He would have stopped hours before and camped for the night, except for a full moon that lit his way well enough for him to see—and for his deep need to be with Leslie. His anxiety at seeing her again made him nervous and jumpy. His palms were hot and clammy, which made carrying his burden all that much more difficult.

He rounded the bend in the road and looked expectantly in the direction of the cabin. There were no lights in the windows, no smoke coming from the chimney. His heart felt like stone, not beating and sinking deep in his chest, as he got the impression that the place was deserted. It was only a little after nine-thirty, and Leslie didn't usually go to bed this early, he calculated quickly. And there'd still be smoke from the fire, unless she hadn't lit one. What if she *couldn't* light the fire? The thought hit him like a low blow to the stomach. What if she'd been out target practicing again or wandered too far into the woods? What if some animal had wandered by, and she'd panicked? He realized the possibilities were endless, even before he dropped the food and started running toward the cabin.

Winded, but still energized with the high doses of adrenaline his body was pumping around inside him, he burst through the cabin door calling Leslie's name. Fumbling in his haste, he finally got a lamp lit only to find that the cabin was indeed empty. He spun around to the door again and was about to go out in search of Leslie, when he spotted a note on the dinette table.

Dear Joe,
I've gone to your neighbor's cabin. I walked ten miles before, I can do it again. I've taken your compass, sleeping bag, and a few other things I'll be needing to camp with. I'll use his

phone to call home, and I'll mail you a check for all the things I'm using. If any of them have sentimental value, I'll be leaving them at your neighbor's, where you can pick them up.

You know, everything you said this morning was true. If you'd said the same thing to me six months ago, I'd have let it roll off my back. Today, however, it hurt. That has to mean something.

I'm sorry for all the trouble I've caused you.

Leslie

P.S. I'll send someone up with a tow truck.

With an angry growl, Joe wadded the note up and threw it on the floor. He wanted her there, in his arms, not out wandering around in the forest feeling sorry for herself. For half a second he was tempted to let her go. She'd come back in a hurry when she discovered his nearest neighbor was a bear that lived in a cave somewhere in the high cavernous peaks between his cabin and the ranger station over forty miles away.

He removed the vest he'd taken with him that morning and reached for his down jacket only to find it was one of the "few other things" she'd taken. At least she'd be warm, he thought disjointedly. Grabbing up the spare flash light and an extra blanket, he blew out the lamp and marched out the door. He'd teach her that running away from her problems was no answer, that running from him would never be tolerated. That they belonged together. And once she'd grasped these lessons, he'd beg for her forgiveness.

"So far, so good," Leslie decreed. She scrutinized her surroundings, her eyes alert to the slightest movement, her ears finely honed to the merest sound. The tall pines stood motionless and seemed to watch over her protectively. The small fire she'd set crackled happily, kept her warm, and gave her light. She was well pleased with her adventure so far.

All day long she'd watched the compass and followed the sun as it rose over her head and settled in the west. All these were signs, she knew, that she was heading in the right direction. West. What she didn't want, more than anything, was to get lost. She was fairly certain Joe wouldn't come looking for her, because she had made a point of telling him that she had a compass and camping equipment. She knew and trusted him well enough to know that if he thought she was out in the forest without any supplies, he'd come after her. He might hate her, but he had an overdeveloped sense of duty and responsibility. So she'd tried to put his mind to rest on that score.

Thinking about him still hurt. Her thoughts seemed to echo in the emptiness she felt. She missed him already. That was strange, she decided. All they ever did was fight it seemed. Still, she did feel all alone, more alone than she had ever felt before. She sighed and rested her chin on her drawn up knees. Max Darkwood wouldn't have said those kind of things to her. Well, not unless he was hurting emotionally and "senselessly lashed out to draw her into his pain, to join him in his sorrow, to draw comfort from her strength" the way he had with Princess Glowing Moon when he found himself madly in love with her, only to discover that it had been her tribe that had scalped his parents when he was fourteen years old. In any case, it was quite understandable in that particular instance, Leslie decided.

And no matter how much he'd hurt her, and even

if he wasn't in love with her, Max would never have let her wander the woods alone. He was a little chauvinistic—well, a lot chauvinistic—but he was also a very sensitive, caring man. He acted tough on the outside, but inside he was gentle and loving. Leslie sighed again. The first thing she was going to do when she got home was write Max Darkwood a letter and tell him he wrote wonderful stories, and that if he was, in actuality, the hero of his books, there was a good chance she was deeply in love with him.

Somewhere nearby a twig snapped. Leslie's head popped up. There was silence, except for the normal night sounds that she had grown accustomed to. Just to make herself feel better, though, she tucked her hand under the sleeping bag she'd wrapped around her legs to feel the reassuring presence of Joe's handgun. She was more familiar with the shotgun, but it was too heavy to pack around for very long. And she was sure the principles of firing the handgun were the same as the shotgun. She felt safe with it cuddled close to her side.

Again there was an odd noise, a rustling of leaves that sounded different from when the wind rustled them. And another snap. Leslie's fingers curled around the gun. She heard a low, throaty growl and more rustling and snapping. The gun came up and went off in one fluid movement. A rock seemed to burst explosively in front of Leslie's wide, frantic eyes, spraying fragments in all directions. The loud, sharp clap echoed through the tree tops and then there was silence. And only then did Leslie realize that she was frightened out of her wits and on the brink of being killed by some wild beast.

A long string of expletives and some of the dirtiest swearwords Leslie had ever heard began to filter through the trees and into her fear-soaked consciousness. They ended with, "Dammit to hell, Leslie, put that damn thing down before you kill me!"

It was Joe. Joe had come after her. Even as angry as he'd been with her and as disgusted as he was with her selfishness, he'd come after her. Her heart was racing wildly and beating an erratic rhythm as she watched him stumble out of the bushes and into her small camp. She tried to go to him. She wanted to throw her arms around him and kiss him until he wasn't angry anymore, but her legs felt like jelly. She wanted to say something, anything, but her tongue turned suddenly spastic, tying itself in knots. So, she had to let Joe do all the talking, and he didn't exactly have Max Darkwood's vocabulary.

"Are you out of your mind? You could have called out and warned me you had a gun. And you never shoot at rocks. Bullets ricochet, you idiot. And what the hell are you doing out here anyway? Feeling sorry for yourself? How come you didn't stay put and hit me with something when I walked through the door? Do you have any idea what kind of danger you're in out here all alone in the middle of nowhere?" He started walking toward her as he shouted, "People with more brains and know-how than you have been known to die up here. Taking off like that was a damned stupid thing to do. I ought to wring your neck," he said as he landed on his knees beside her, his eyes wild with fury and passion. His hands cupped her face, and she swallowed hard, thinking he might very well carry out his threat. But she didn't move. "I ought to . . . and I will, if you ever leave me again."

His words slowed and softened, and the passion began to consume the ferociousness in his gaze as he cast it wondrously over her face. Without warning, he lowered his head and his lips covered her mouth. His tongue was unyielding as it drove between her teeth and took possession of her senses. Joe's kiss was long and fiery and heartfelt. It shook the mountain and made Leslie tremble with its power and depth. Her world began to reel out of focus, and her hands automatically reached out to Joe for support. Joe winced and sucked in a sharp breath.

"What is it? What's wrong?" she asked through the haze of her jumbled emotions.

"Nothing. Kiss me again," he murmured, his lips moving against hers, hardly losing contact as he spoke. "Forgive me and kiss me again."

"Oh, Joe." She sighed, her spirits soaring. Her hand passed along his shoulder, enjoying the feel of the power he possessed. Then suddenly her fingertips encountered a warm stickiness, and she instinctively pulled them away. A soft cry of shock escaped her as she stared at her fingers in horror. "You're bleeding," she said with a gasp.

"I'll live. Kiss me."

"What happened? Why? My God, Joe, your shirt is covered with blood."

"You shot me. Kiss me, and I'll forgive you."

"But—" He silenced her with his mouth.

"No, Joe. You'll bleed to death," she said, pushing him away, trying to calm the sick terror that beset her as she began to unbutton his shirt. "I can't believe I did this. I finally fall in love with somebody, and then I shoot him. I need to get into therapy."

"Relax. It's a flesh wound, a scratch. I'm going to die a much worse death if you don't kiss me again. . . . What did you just say?" he asked, his grasp stilling her hands, his demanding look dispelling some of the confusion and agitation in her mind with its insistence.

Leslie hesitated. "When?"

"Just now."

Mentally she had to rewind her recording of the past few minutes. When it came back loud and clear that she'd actually said, out loud, that she loved him, it was almost as big a shock to her as it was to him. Well, maybe not quite as big, she decided. Hadn't she felt all along that there was something special about him, about him and her together. There was most surely a devastating attraction between them, but there was more. She'd never cared what someone else thought of her, not enough to want to please him. She'd never really wanted to make anyone but herself happy. But she wanted Joe to be happy. With or without her, she wanted him to be happy. She wanted to know him in every sense, wanted to please him in any way she could, wanted to be with him indoors or out, in the city or on the mountainside. There was a sense of rightness about her feelings. Joe was the man she'd waited all her life for. She had no proof, no facts, no specific reasons, she just knew it to be true.

With all the confidence of a woman who knew what she was doing, Leslie looked into Joe's deep green eyes and whispered, "I said I love you."

A slow gentle smile crossed his lips while he sat looking at her as if she were a miracle worker.

She gave him a quick, self-conscious peck on the mouth as she rose up on her knees to peel away his shirt. She felt his hands working the buttons along the front of her own shirt and tried to ignore him as she pulled his T-shirt away from his wound. "I'm so sorry," she said anxiously, slipping her fingers into the tear in the cotton and making it larger. "I didn't mean to shoot you. I thought you were an animal."

"I feel like an animal," Joe said as he removed the

flannel shirt from over her arms. "I want you so much, Leslie. I need you so badly."

Leslie pulled on the material of his T-shirt until it began to tear. Through her own T-shirt, she felt Joe's mouth cover the tip her breast and begin to suck. A weakening wave of ecstasy rolled over her, again and again, until she was hard put to keep from falling limply over his shoulder. "Oh, please," she said, moaning. "Let me finish this. I think it's stopped bleeding, but you really ought to have something over it to protect it."

Joe stopped only long enough to remove her T-shirt, while she ripped his in half and off his body. He was cupping her breasts and pulling her closer before she could find a clean corner of the cloth with which to bandage his wound. Feebly she pressed the shirt to his shoulder and was vaguely relieved to see that he had, indeed, stopped bleeding. Joe's lips moved lower, teasing and calculating. His fingers played with the buttons on her jeans until he could slide them down over her hips. Leslie slipped her fingers into his thick dark hair and pressed him closer to her as he laved her navel with his tongue. With her other hand, she fought valiantly to keep the dressing in place on his shoulder, while she tried not to lean too heavily on it for balance. His hands gripped her waist as he moved lower and lower to wreak havoc on her senses.

Intuitively her body seemed to know what to do. It moved closer to Joe, knowing he'd protect her and keep her safe in her mindlessness. Her heart matched its rhythm to his, and they shared their life's breaths as they fell together into a parallel world, where only ungovernable desire and delight existed and profound pleasure reigned supreme.

Leslie's hand roamed slowly over the rolling knolls and valleys across Joe's chest, and she traced the trail of coarse, dark hair all the way to its end. Joe's soft groan rumbled in her ear as it lay pressed against his chest. His arms tightened around her naked body, and he rolled toward her, out of the path of her nomadic fingers.

He came up on one elbow and looked down into her face. She'd never seen an expression quite like his now. He looked almost boyish, full of happiness and hope and contentment. She recognized the emotions easily, as they reflected her own like a mirror.

She shivered briefly when he lifted the covers away and revealed her body to the glowing firelight. She was warmed again as his gaze caressed and cherished every visible inch of her. Wrapping the blanket around her, shielding her from the cool night air once more, he let his hand slide from her neck to her belly in a most proprietary way. "This body was made for loving. So soft and responsive," he uttered as if in awe.

"Joe," she said, urgently needing to make everything between them as perfect as their lovemaking had been. "I did read your books. All of them. I smuggled them out every afternoon and read them cover to cover."

Joe frowned and gave an amazed little chuckle. "Why'd you feel you had to sneak around to read them? I wanted you to read them. I wanted your opinion on them."

"That's just it. I couldn't give you an opinion, aside from the fact that I thought you wrote wonderfully. I knew nothing about the things you wrote about. I mean, not enough to have an opinion on them anyway. You were right this morning. I've had my head buried in the sand, in my own little world for so long, I had no idea of what was going on around me. I was ashamed to let you know or even have you guess at the truth. I didn't want you to think badly of me."

"Humph. I'm surprised you cared what I thought at all. I've been such an ass to you. And it doesn't matter that you and I don't have the same interests—"

"But that's not the point, Joe. It wasn't just your respect I was afraid of losing. I had to get some of my own back. I always thought I was so smart, that I had everything figured out and under control. And all along I was standing knee deep in confusion and chaos. I was just too stupid and selfish to open my eyes and see it. I can't tell you how awful it is to wake up one morning and discover you have no life, that nothing you've been doing means anything."

"But Leslie, honey, that's not what's important. What is important is that you did wake up. Some people never do."

She thought over what he'd said in silence, aware of the solidness of his hand on her stomach and of the words he spoke. He might speak gruffly and show a hard exterior, but inside he was stable and understanding, caring and gentle and giving. "You know," she said, tracing his cheekbone with the tip of her finger, "I like you very much when you act like this. In some ways you remind me very much of Max Darkwood."

Joe laughed. "You really have a thing for him, don't you?"

"Well, it's not as big as the thing I have for you, but he certainly finishes a close second place. He's sweet and gentle and tender. He's honest and loving and faithful. Max is someone you know you can trust."

"Yes, but can Max kiss you like this . . . ? Or touch you here . . . or here . . . or make you feel that? No? What about this?" Joe proceeded to stir her emotions and drive her senses wild with a need only he could satisfy. "If you were to ask me," he murmured against her throat, "I'd have to say you made the best choice. Max could never love you like I do."

Long after dawn had pledged itself to the day, Leslie and Joe lay under the warming rays of the sun, oblivious to their nakedness—except when it suited their whims. Then it was very handy. For hours they did nothing but lie in each other's arms and talk. Sometimes their chatter was nonsensical, but more often than not, it was autobiographical as they tried to encapsulate their lifetimes into small doses for the other to ingest. They felt an urgency to know all there was to know about the other, to share secrets and dreams, to bond deeply and irrevocably.

All the while, Joe didn't seem able to keep his hands off her. Always touching, always stroking, his hands were reverent and indulgent. Leslie had never felt so cherished or adored. He was as free and familiar with her body as he was with his own. Deprived of such closeness in the past, and not realizing it until now, she soaked it up thirstily like a dry sponge, wanting more.

Leslie leaned over Joe and kissed him softly, simply because she wanted to. "Do you suppose we should get going? Or shall we sleep here again tonight?"

"Did we sleep here last night?" Joe asked with a yawn. "I don't remember sleeping."

Leslie laughed at her own recollections of the previous night. "Let me rephrase that. Can you afford any more time away from your work?"

Throwing his arms around her and rolling over on

top of her, Joe looked down at Leslie with regret in his eyes. "No, I can't. But I'd much rather stay here with you. Although," he said, his mood lightening, "there's a lot to be said for beds and food and some of the other comforts back at the cabin." He pulled a dry leaf from Leslie's tangle of dark hair and grinned at her.

"Does your shoulder hurt much?"

"No. I've been too distracted to pay much attention to it."

From overhead, came a high-pitched screech that resounded for miles over the valleys and mountaintops. The sky was a clear, true blue, empty, but for a lone bird that stretched and soared across the vast openness as if it were lord paramount over all other living creatures.

"I guess we'll have to go now. Archibald has found us," Joe said, leaning back on his arms to watch the bird circling above them, climbing higher and higher with every rotation. "And he doesn't look happy to see us."

"Archibald?"

"Leslie, honey, you are looking at one of your national birds. That is a bald eagle, hence, his name. He and his wife have taken to nesting in the vicinity. We met last year."

The bird seemed huge, even from a distance. She couldn't see his white head, but she could make out white tail feathers. Either way, she had to take the identification on faith, because she wouldn't know a bald eagle unless it had a nameplate attached to it. Whatever the species, there was something definitely thrilling about seeing him, she decided as she watched the bird glide through the sky. At one point Leslie felt the bird ought to flap his wings to keep up his speed, but he didn't. She found herself holding her breath as he continued to float on the air without effort.

"Isn't he wonderful?" she whispered.

"Mm." Joe, too, had his gaze fixed on the eagle. "I was really glad to see him again this year. They don't always come back to nest in the same place every year, and they almost never build their nests this low. They like the higher altitudes. Last year the ranger said there wasn't another pair of them for two or three hundred miles."

They watched in silence until the bird gracefully flew out of sight. It was like the finale to a wondrous and magical episode in their lives, a signal that it was time to pack up and go back to reality.

"Tell you what," Joe said, as he tucked in his shirt and kicked Leslie's other moccasin closer so she could reach it. "I'm nearly finished with this report I've been working on. I'll take a day off, and we'll go up and check out the eagle's nest, see how many babies they had this year. Last year there were two. I've been hoping the little ones would fly in to see their folks this summer, but I haven't seen them."

"I'd like that . . . I think." She cast him a dubious glance. The mountains were growing on her, there was no doubt about that. But she'd never be the gung ho, outdoorsy type. Nature wasn't in her nature. She was about to explain this to Joe, when something else he'd said triggered a response in her mind. "I thought you were working on another book. What's this about a report?"

"Actually that's what I wanted you to think, so you'd leave me alone. But the truth is, I'm working on a labor of love, and I won't get a penny for it. Although there is a thread of a chance it may save my cabin."

"I don't understand."

"There's a development company in Denver that's

planning on putting a ski run through my cabin. Since I lease it from the state, there's not a whole lot I can do about it alone. But I've joined forces with an environmental group. They want to save the inner Rockies as wilderness land and keep the ski resorts and campgrounds limited to the outer, lateral mountains."

"How does it look? Can they make that happen?" Leslie asked, hoping desperately that the sinking feeling in her stomach and the salty, nauseated feeling of knowing the truth could somehow be changed by Joe's inside knowledge.

Joe shook his head and something pierced her heart. The pain and guilt and hopelessness were more than she could bear. She opened her mouth to tell Joe the truth of what she'd done, but he was already speaking again. "I think it's been pretty much decided. All the reports and environmental impact studies are done, and the permits are granted by the state long before the development company actually takes over and puts money into a project. But this group has been protesting all along, so they've been granted an appeals interview with a review officer of the forest service. They're hoping they can come up with enough support or adequate evidence to get the whole decision thrown into the district court. Then, depending on the judge, there might be a chance."

"How does it look though? Do you think they can do it?" she asked anxiously.

"Wilderness doesn't bring in a lot of revenue for the state, Les. The group needs a miracle."

"Your report?"

"No. It's not going to make much difference, I just don't know how else to help. We'll send it to other naturalist groups around the country and deliver it to the review officer, but it's not going to make or break our case. You ready? Got everything?" Leslie nodded, in too much turmoil to speak. "Ah, don't look so down in the mouth, sweetheart. I know hiking isn't your favorite pastime, but you didn't really get all that far from the cabin. Two, three miles, tops."

Leslie frowned. "Are you joking? I walked all day yesterday and only went three miles?"

Nine

"Ah." Leslie moaned in ecstasy. "A little lower. Oh. yes. Right there."

"Here?" Joe asked as he leaned over Leslie's shoulder and planted a kiss on the top of her head.

The fire flared and crackled noisily. Its golden light glowed warmly over Leslie's skin and danced in her ebony hair. Joe's bare chest was cast into angular shadows that seemed to move and change shape as he used his strength to ease Leslie's aching need. She turned her head to the light, and Joe smiled at the euphoric expression that had relaxed her tense features of moments ago. "Feel good?" he asked in a low, soothing voice.

"Mm."

"Want me to stop?"

"No," she murmured, barely conscious. "But if you're getting tired, you can."

Joe laughed. "Listen, this beats chopping wood all to pieces. I just thought you might want to move this back rub over to the bed. You're getting pruney, and the water's not even warm anymore," he said, shaking Leslie's tepid bath water from his hands and reaching for her towel.

"And you have to get back to work," she added for

him, since he wasn't likely to say it. Joe was so different, she mused dreamily. In the past few days he seemed to have undergone a metamorphosis from the crabby, temperamental writer, to a gentle, considerate lover, whose uppermost thoughts were focused on her alone. Even his writing seemed to take a backseat to her needs and desires.

At first it had been a heady experience. She'd never held so much power over another human before. Nor had anyone ever had such an effect on her. She loved Joe. She loved him better the more she knew him. She loved him more with each passing day. And with each day she learned that her power over him wasn't something she wanted to abuse. The fact that he would spend his time with her doing whatever she wanted to do instead of locking himself up in the cabin to write wasn't what she wanted. Well, she loved it actually, but not at the expense of his first love, his writing. She was careful to keep to the routine he'd set up when they first arrived at the cabin so he could work. She did this unselfishly and without resentment because she loved him and because his mountain needed him more than she did at the moment. "I think I will get out now. I feel much better."

"You didn't have to do all the laundry today. You could have done it in stages. Jeans today, what few T-shirts I have left tomorrow, whatever's not done the day after that. Then again, you're not exactly a halfway person, are you? It's all or nothing, right?"

"I'm afraid so. And believe me, this isn't the first time I've been punished for being that way." She stood stiffly and let Joe wrap her tightly in a soft yellow towel, held securely in place by his loving arms.

"I'm not complaining. I like your tenacity, the way you stick to things. When you say you love me, I know you don't just think you do, you feel it, or you wouldn't say it. And you'll see it through to the end, wherever it leads us, because that's the way you are."

Leslie turned her head so she could place a tender kiss on his mouth. "I do love you."

The now familiar look of contentment and boyish happiness softened his gaze and gently curved his lips as he regarded her adoringly. "I know you do," he said before he kissed her in a way that revealed the fathomless depths of his own emotions.

When he released her so she could get dressed for bed and he had returned to his little computer, Leslie couldn't shake the feeling of dissatisfaction that crept into her heart. Joe had said he loved her only once and that had been in the throes of passion. She didn't doubt his love, exactly. His whole attitude toward her was a statement of deep affection. The way he looked at her, his kisses, his touch, other things he said, told of his love for her. But he never came right out and said it.

While she attached the hose that would drain the water in the small bathtub into the kitchen sink, she wondered if Joe's previous lover was the cause of his reluctance to say I love you. The woman had hurt him badly, and Leslie, for the first time in her life, actually hated someone she didn't even know. Then again, love made you think and do and feel a lot of strange and irrational things. And, happily, Leslie wouldn't have it any other way.

Had she ever been more satisfied with her life, she wondered, as she crawled up onto the middle of the bed with her next Darkwood novel to wait for Joe. She didn't think so. She'd never felt more whole. It was wonderful to be the Leslie she was and the Leslie she'd always wanted to be at the same time.

She and Joe had spent hours discussing a variety

of subjects. Those she wasn't well informed on, she asked Joe about. He would explain or give his opinion without reproach or disapproval. Those she was familiar with she spoke freely and intelligently about and, she suspected, had amazed Joe with how truly bright she was. Neither one of them had given an accurate account of themselves when they first met, she supposed.

She'd amazed herself quite frequently of late as to how attuned she had become to so many new experiences. Joe was an obvious one, but even the mountain seemed to touch her—and not always with guilt. She found she didn't have to be a jock to enjoy the mountains and the out-of-doors. Just sitting in the shade by the woodshed, she would find herself in such a quiet, peaceful state of mind, she wondered how anyone survived in the hubbub of the city. She still was leery of the animals, but she enjoyed the birds immensely. She was almost to the point of wishing that she and Joe could stay together in the mountains forever.

Part of that wish, however, stemmed from shame and cowardice. She hadn't told Joe of her involvement with the development company that eventually would destroy his mountain and his cabin. She wanted to be truthful. It was her nature to be honest and up-front. But the words she needed to tell Joe didn't seem to exist in her vocabulary. She'd tried to tell him, more than once, but short of simply blurting it out, there didn't seem to be an easy way. She found it preferable to think that the right words would suddenly occur to her at the right moment and tried not to dwell on it too much. But the fact remained ever present and very heavy in her heart and mind.

Then again, if they were never rescued, there was

a good chance she'd have to do the laundry again, and her back might not hold out.

"Now which one are you reading?" Flat on her stomach, her mind wandering, Leslie was startled to hear Joe's question and feel his long, half-naked body slide over hers. He wrapped his arms around her from behind, his chin coming to rest on her left shoulder. He kissed her cheek and nuzzled her neck. Her stomach muscles coiled into a tight knot of desire, as her heart picked up its pace and began to throb excitedly in her throat.

"Ah . . . this one is about . . ." It was hard for her to think and speak simultaneously when Joe's hands were moving on a predetermined path to his ultimate goal, that of making her totally senseless with need for him. It was especially difficult when he didn't play fair and used his tongue and mouth to torment an ultrasensitive area on her neck. He knew every nook and cranny on her body by now, and he obviously had no scruples when it came to getting what he wanted. What they both wanted, she admitted to herself with a wily smile. "Ah . . . Spit and Max have just . . . um . . . found the two orphans, whose parents were— "

"Were killed by marauding Indians," Joe finished for her, slipping to one side so his lips could get to the opening of the night shirt she was wearing. "If I tell you how it ends, will you put the damn thing down and let me make love to you?"

"Don't you dare tell me how it ends. He hasn't even met the woman yet." She glanced at Joe and was going to pretend to keep on reading, but something in his eyes caught her attention. "What's so funny?"

"You."

Leslie's eyebrows rose disdainfully, as she failed to see the humor.

"I never would have imagined that you'd end up a Darkwood junkie. His readers are usually male. He'll be very hard to live with once he develops a female following as well. I'm not sure he can handle hordes of women throwing themselves at him for his autograph."

"You know him?" she asked, ignoring his innuendo about her hero.

"Why else would I have all his books? You don't think I'd actually choose to read that junk do you? He gives them to me."

"You really know him? Personally?"

"Yep. And if you're real nice to me, I'll get him to give you an autograph," he said enticingly as he slowly ran his index finger from her bottom lip down the middle of the V of her shirt to the first secured button. He looked up at Leslie with a very evil glint in his eyes.

"That's blackmail."

"I know." He confidently slipped the first button through its hole, while his other hand slithered knowingly up her thigh and under the tail of her shirt.

"I can't believe you'd stoop to this. I'm . . . ah . . . I feel backed into a corner here," she said, turning slightly so she could touch him, feel him, use him as an anchor to keep from spinning off into nothingness, as her mind grew dark and thoughtless. Ripples of sensation became torrent waves of excitement. "I feel so helpless."

"I know." Joe's voice was a hoarse groan of desire and passion as he covered her mouth with his, taking what he knew to be his alone. Taking it, not greedily, but slowly and with relish until he had consumed it all. Then just as painstakingly he gave it back, knowing Leslie to be a safe vessel in which to keep it, trusting her with all that was precious to him . . . their love for each other.

Emotionally drugged and exhausted, they lay in each other's arms. Without a care or complaint, they simply were happy to be alive and in love.

"Roll over," Joe said suddenly.

"Why?" Leslie asked lethargically.

"Trust me. Just roll over and don't look."

She did as he requested and fought hard not to peek as she felt him leave the bed. She listened. He was at his desk for a mere second and then back in bed, bouncing the springs violently with his exuberance. Cool air prickled her skin when he drew the covers off, exposing her nakedness.

"I'm cold," she complained weakly, anxious to see what he was up to.

"Shh. Trust me. I'm a man of my word. I always keep my promises."

"What are you doing?" she squeaked as she felt him at her hip . . . writing on her? She twisted around to get a look just in time to see him underline it with a long zigzag that went all the way down her bottom. "Wha . . ."

"There. You see. I told you I'd get you his autograph."

"You mean, you're . . ."

Joe smiled smugly. "Max supports me in a style that even a yuppie like you wouldn't think was too shabby. Which then allows me to write the kinds of books that mean something to me but, regrettably, don't sell well."

"You mean all this time—" She stopped short. All the time she'd been falling in love with Max Darkwood and falling in love with Joe Bonner, she'd been falling in love with the same man, over and over and over again. Now that she stopped to think about it, she felt incredibly stupid for not having seen it earlier. The hero was so like Joe: Tough and brassy on the outside and as soft as a marshmallow on the inside. Brave and honest and reliable and . . . honest? "Why didn't you tell me?"

"What? And have you falling in love with me because of my money?" When she began to sputter righteously, he laughed. "Think back, Leslie. When I first brought you here, I wasn't even sure I wanted you around. I wasn't sure I wanted you to know anything about me. But I do now. I want you to know all about me. And I want to know all about you. I don't want there to be any secrets between us. Ever."

Leslie's throat grew dry and tight. She felt as if she were chewing cotton balls. Her heart beat sluggishly and her stomach seemed to have become a bottomless pit of burning acid. Joe was apparently satisfied that there were no more secrets between them. He curled himself around her, holding her close, giving every indication he was about to go to sleep. But Leslie knew her night's rest wasn't going to come as easily. She had a secret that had to be told, had to be told soon, or she'd lose the only thing that really meant anything to her. Joe.

Before she got out of bed the next morning, she vowed that she'd tell Joe the truth about her and the mountain. She wouldn't close her eyes on another day without telling him. Not that they'd been closed all that long the night before. She had spent most of those dark hours vacillating between her need to tell Joe the truth and the consequences she might have to pay if she did. Since he was bound to find out sooner or later, and her compulsion to tell him was so great that it was depriving her of sleep, she decided to get it over with. She'd find the words to make him understand. She had to.

The clothes she'd washed the day before had hung

out all through the night to dry and had gathered dew in the early morning, which meant that Leslie had to leave them out until the sun was well overhead to redry. Even then the jeans remained damp to the touch. She gathered these first and took them into the cabin to dry, one by one, in front of the fire.

While Joe worked on the nearly finished report for the forest-service hearing, Leslie gathered the rest of the laundry that hung from the limbs of trees and lay neatly over the tops of bushes. "Joe," she said aloud, practicing her words for the next time he looked up from his keyboard. "I have something I want to tell you. I have something I need to tell you." She shook her head. "Joe, I've changed a lot since we first met. But there's something I need to tell you about. Something I did before I knew better." Again she shook her head. "Joe. Remember the night we met, and you asked me what I was doing up here in the mountains? Well, I never did give you an answer. It really hasn't come up since then. But I think now would be a good time to tell you." Her last attempt sounded good to her.

She began folding a T-shirt that was scented with clean, fresh air and only slightly less rigid than a piece of cardboard. She was going to miss her fabric softener in the weeks to come, she ruminated. She laid it in the box with the others and leaned up against the large boulder it had been draped over to decide how she would proceed with her explanation to Joe.

As much as he loved her, she didn't expect to escape unscathed by Joe's temper, but maybe she could mollify him by getting him to understand. She kicked at the loose rocks that littered the ground around the boulder as words came to mind and were rejected, one right after another.

A deep sigh of frustration escaped her as she turned

back to the laundry. Maybe she could write him a letter, she thought, as she moved around the huge stone to reach another shirt. She'd always been able to express herself better on paper than face to face with another human being. She moved her foot to stabilize her balance as she reached high for a last piece of clothing on the rock. A twig from one of the surrounding bushes slipped up inside the leg of her jeans. It scratched a little, and she shook her leg to rid herself of it, but it wouldn't come loose. Grabbing at the shirt she'd been reaching for, she came down on firm ground and bent to remove the branch, only to discover that it wasn't a branch at all.

Long, tubular, and bent at an odd angle, nearly three feet of black and brown snake hung out from under the hem of her pants. A convulsion of fear and repulsion rippled through her body before her mouth opened to emit a blood-curdling scream. In that same instant, panic seized her and she snatched at the tail of the snake to pull it away. With one fierce, ripping motion she pulled at it. She experienced a sharp, piercing pain above her ankle that brought forth another desperate cry of horror, before the viper came free. She flung it several feet away and sank to the ground holding her ankle, her pulse racing, her breathing rapid and shallow, tears welling and rolling down from her eyes.

"Oh, lord. Oh, lord. Oh, lord," she cried, frantic with terror and the knowledge that she was going to die from the snakebite.

"Leslie!" Joe's face was a mask of fright and worry as he ran from the cabin toward her. "What is it? What's wrong?" he asked, falling to his knees beside her.

"My leg. A snake. It bit me." Her sobs strained her words and caused her to breathe irregularly. Her hands were shaking uncontrollably as Joe wordlessly removed them from around her ankle and pushed her pant leg up to expose the wound. There were two puncture sites, each oozing blood but not copiously. Already the site was swollen and inflamed and tender to the touch.

"Damn," Joe muttered under his breath. His eyes, when they met Leslie's, were grave and tormented with grief. "Listen to me, Leslie," he said sternly, using his voice to break through her hysteria. "You're going to be fine. Do you hear me? You'll be fine. I'm going in—"

"No! Don't leave me," she pleaded. Tears blurred her vision. She reached out blindly and took hold of his shirt sleeve to keep him near her.

"I have to. Just for a minute. I have to call for help."

"No. There's no phone. I'm going to die. Please, don't leave me."

"There's a shortwave radio in one of the cabinets. It's been there all along. Let go, sweetheart, we can't waste any more time." He pulled away from her grasping hands and didn't take the time to look back at her when she called out his name. There'd be time enough to comfort her after he'd called for help— nothing but time—and each precious minute that was wasted would be vital to her life.

Little had changed by the time he came hurrying toward her with a blanket over one arm and a first aid kit in his hands. She was still crying but quietly, mournfully, helplessly. She was leaning with her back against the boulder, holding her bent leg just below the knee.

"They'll be here soon. Half hour, forty-five minutes tops," Joe said. "The ranger said to keep you as quiet as possible and," he paused, looking around as if he were trying to find something, "I need to kill the snake so we can take it with us to make sure you get the right antivenin. Do you remember where it went?" he asked gently, kneeling beside her and covering her with the blanket.

"No. Stay away from it, Joe." She sat up in her agitation and took a firm grip on his arm to keep him from going after it. "Stay with me."

"Shh." Joe gently pushed her back against the rock and tucked the blanket around her shoulders again. "I won't leave you. I just want to make sure it's not around anymore. Where did it go?"

"I threw it. I threw it over there." She pointed out the direction for him and cried out again when he stood. "No. Don't. You might get bitten."

"I need to check, baby. I'll be careful. Don't worry." He stealthily moved off into the bushes beside the stone, pushing the brush back as he went.

"Do you see it? Is it still there?" Leslie called out when she could no longer see him.

"Not yet."

"Why didn't you tell me about the radio? Why haven't you used it before now? We could have been rescued days ago." The mental shock was beginning to wear off, but the physical aftermath was evident as she began to shiver even though she knew she wasn't cold. Her leg ached and throbbed. Her ankle grew tight and hard to move as the swelling continued.

"I didn't tell you about it," she heard a rustling of leaves as he paused, "because I didn't want to. I didn't want you to know."

She could hear him returning and turned her head expectantly. "But why?"

"I didn't want you to go," he said simply, back at her side, tying a knot in a plastic bread bag.

"Is that it? Is it dead?" she asked, knowing the answer as she watched the snake's blood pooling in the bottom of the bag.

"Well, I put my boot on its head and cut it in half.

The damn thing better be dead," he said with a wry smile. He came down on one knee and began to put a clean, loose dressing over her wound.

Leslie nodded numbly, still staring at the bag. She was glad the thing was dead. She would have liked to have killed it herself. Recalling the question she had been about to ask, she said, "But you hated me in the beginning. Why didn't you call someone to come and get me then?"

Joe laughed unexpectedly. "I'd sure like to know where you got the idea that I hated you. This is the second time you've accused me of that." He sat down beside her, looping an arm around her shoulder, pulling her close and holding her near him. "I think I was in love with you the first time I looked down and found you lying under me. I didn't want to be, but I was. I could have called the ranger station that first night, but since you were on vacation and no one was likely to worry about you for a couple of weeks, I decided to keep you for a while, to see if I could talk myself out of wanting you so badly. That was a little presumptuous of me, huh?"

"Yeah, a little," she said, wanting to sound angry and indignant, while all she managed to do was smile and laugh softly. "So, why were you so nasty? Haven't you heard that old saying about catching more bees with honey?"

"That's what made me so mad. I didn't want to catch you. We're nothing alike. We have nothing in common. And there I was, crazy about you, sitting on my hands to keep them away from you. It was very frustrating."

"Serves you right. You were awfully mean to me," she said, growing drowsy. The pain in her leg was now a tingling sensation, as if the limb had gone to sleep. It was the rest of her body that ached at present, especially when she moved. Her eyelids grew heavy as she tried to remain motionless in Joe's warm embrace. "What made you decide to love me in spite of all our differences?"

"I don't know. Suddenly it didn't matter that we were different. Maybe it was better that way. Maybe we were meant to offset each other, to compensate for each other's faults. Like what's his name . . . Jack Sprat and his wife. Remember that guy?"

"Mm," she moaned sleepily, trying to remember if she'd forgotten to tell Joe something important. Had she gotten all the laundry folded, she wondered vaguely. "His wife was fat," she muttered.

She felt the vibrations in Joe's chest as he laughed quietly and hugged her tightly. "All that matters is that we love each other and that we're happy together."

His loving gesture brought a groan of misery to her lips. "I'm not feeling well, Joe."

"Does it hurt?"

"It's asleep, but I'm a little sick to my stomach, and I hurt all over."

"Hang on, sweetheart. They'll be here soon, and you'll be fine. I promise."

Leslie fought to keep her eyes open, to stay alert. She was missing something important. What was it? "I love you, Joe," she said, knowing that was something vital that he had to be aware of.

"I love you, too, Leslie. Very much."

"What have I forgotten to tell you?"

"Your true age?" Joe knew how old she was. She could remember the night he'd teased her about it and she'd had to show him her driver's license. She suspected he was trying to keep the mood light to dispel the gravity of the situation, but she wasn't in a carefree mood. Still, her mind seemed to leap at the chance to go off on a tangent. It began to recall all sorts of special moments the two of them had shared in the past two weeks.

In a dreamlike state of mind it was easy to conjure up the day Joe had worked eight hours straight on his report and then chased her around the woodshed because she'd stolen all his computer batteries to get him to stop for a while. And the day he'd found her asleep under the big pine tree by the garden. He'd made her a crown of the pretty little blue flowers that grew along the forest floor to wear in her hair. And the day they went to see the eagle's nest. The sun had shone brightly and the mountain had been so beautiful that day.

"Joe. That's it," she said, sitting up abruptly to face him, grimacing as her body objected to this burst of activity. "I need to tell you about the mountain. I need for you to understand that I didn't mean to do it. It's all my fault, and I'd change it if I could, but I'm afraid it's hopeless at this stage."

"Leslie, honey, what are you talking about? Lie back down. You're getting too excited. You need to stay quiet and calm. Please. Lie down. We can talk later."

"No. I can't close my eyes until I tell you. If I hadn't been so self-centered and ambitious this might not have happened. I had no idea it was so beautiful."

"Sweetheart, you're not making sense right now. Just rest. We'll talk later. Shh . . . hear that?" They both paused to listen to the steady thumping sound that was advancing toward them rapidly. "It's them. You're going to be fine, baby."

"But, Joe. I have to tell you. It was me all along. I'm the one who destroyed the mountain. I need you to understand and find some way to forgive me."

"I do. I forgive you. I love you. Now rest. Please." Leslie got the distinct impression that he would have said anything to shut her up and settle her down again. The helicopter was soon visible, and Joe was wrapping her tightly in the blanket, covering her face with his body to keep the flying dirt away from her.

Leslie was tired. She'd tried her best to tell him, and it seemed to appease her conscience. Her eyes drifted closed, and she entrusted her spirit to the fates. She took comfort in the darkness that rose up to meet her.

Places, faces, and voices drifted in and out of her consciousness. Bright lights, her father's voice, the hazy image of a stranger's face came to her and then quickly were gobbled up in the darkness. At some point she woke to find Joe asleep in a chair beside her. The lighting was dim and gloomy, but she could make out his features. She drew comfort from his peaceful presence and closed her eyes once more to sleep.

"I called Beth again," Leslie heard her mother saying. "As long as Leslie is going to be fine, there's no reason for them to cut their honeymoon short to come home, is there? She won't appreciate us making a big fuss out of this when she wakes up, you know."

"No. No," her father agreed. "I think you're right. That was a good idea. There's nothing for Beth to do here but get on Leslie's nerves. She can do that after the honeymoon."

Beth won't get on my nerves, Leslie said in the back of her mind. Well, not the way she used to. And it's okay if you want to make a fuss over me. I want you to. It's your way of showing me your love. I need love. It makes life worth living. It puts a value on every second that passes. I love the both of you. And I love Beth. And from now on, you're going to know I do. Because I'm going to tell you and show you in every way I can.

"Did the doctor say when she'd be waking up?" her mother asked. "I'm dying to find out what she was doing up in those mountains with that young man."

"Now, Mother," Stan Rothe cautioned his wife. "She's a big girl."

"I know, dear. I just can't understand why she hasn't opened her eyes yet."

"Maybe she's just lying there enjoying the sound of your voices," Leslie said, a sleepy smile spreading slowly across her face as she opened her eyes.

"Oh, darling. You are awake. How are you feeling?"

"I'm not sure yet, Mother. Good, I guess. And I'm glad to see you." She returned her mother's kiss on the cheek and added a hug for good measure. "Hi, Dad."

"Hi, honey." He took his turn at Leslie's cheek, then stepped back to study her intently as if he could sense there was something different about her. "Well? Are you going to keep us on tenterhooks, or would you like to tell us how you came to be bitten by a snake?"

Leslie smiled wryly. "It's not exactly something you'd expect to happen to me of all people, is it?"

"No. You've always been the original hothouse orchid in my book. When did you develop this interest in unpasteurized air?"

"Didn't Joe explain it to you? You met him, didn't you?"

"Yes, dear, we met him," her mother said. Leslie picked up on a hesitation in her voice and instantly was wary.

"Where is Joe?"

Her parents looked at each other meaningfully, and Leslie's heart began to skip beats. "Where is he?" she asked again.

Stan Rothe shook his head, searching for words.

"We don't know, honey. He called us last night and told us what happened. Everything seemed fine when we met him here. We had dinner together downstairs in the cafeteria. We talked. He talked. It got late, and he told us to go home, that he'd stay with you until morning. But by the time we got back, he was gone. The nurse gave us this to give to you."

Leslie took the envelope her father pulled out of his breast pocket, staring at it in confusion and dread. Intuitively she knew that it was all she had left of her time in the mountains, in the little cabin, in Joe's heart. Something had gone wrong, or he would still be at her side.

"What did the three of you talk about?" she asked, sounding almost indifferent. She was filled with a sense of foreboding, she knew in her heart what they had talked about.

"You mostly," her mother said cautiously, knowing how protective her daughter was of her privacy. "He seemed to know so much about you already that we assumed he was special to you and that it was okay to talk to him about you."

Leslie smiled weakly at her mother, realizing what a difficult daughter she'd been for so many years. "He is someone special. And it was okay."

Mrs. Rothe relaxed visibly and went on. "We talked about how strange it was for you to be in the mountains. And he didn't seem to know why you were there either, so then we told him what a peculiar creature you are with all your do's and don'ts. He seemed to think them very funny and even knew about some of them. We talked about your job, and Dad and I told him how proud of you we are. Honestly, dear, I can't think of a thing we said that might have upset him. He seemed fine when we left, and the nurse said he stayed until he knew you'd be all right."

Leslie shook her head, looking at the envelope in her hands. "It wasn't you, Mother. It was me."

Her fingers automatically tore at the paper that covered the fate of her hopes, her dreams, and the love Joe had given her. The missive was short:

The reason history keeps repeating itself is because no one was listening the first time. I can't afford to make the same mistake twice. One liar in my lifetime was more than enough.

Ten

Three weeks later, Leslie Rothe, data-research analyst for the Darby Development Company walked into a conference room in the state government building in downtown Denver. Her high heels clicked loudly on the old stone floors, announcing her arrival. She stood tall and proud. Her linen suit was flawless and wrinkle free. Every dark hair on her head was curled to perfection. Her face was shrouded with an expression of indifference. For every intent and purpose, she appeared to consider this hearing before the forest service review officer a trifling inconvenience.

Appearances were, indeed, deceptive. Inside she was racked with pain. Her makeup covered the dark shadows under her eyes caused by weeks without adequate sleep. She had all but begged Nathan Darby not to send her to the hearing, especially after being informed that it had been moved from Jack Sullivan's office to a conference room to allow for the large group of protesters they were expecting. Joe Bonner was bound to be one of them, and the mere thought of having to face him again was pure torture to the lacerations that still lay open and raw in her heart. For days now she had labored under the misery and torment of knowing that she would see him once more and that he would look at her through the eyes of a man who hated her.

She couldn't bring herself to pick him out of the crowd as she walked to the table at the front of the room. Nathan Darby was already there. A clean-cut, smooth-talking business tycoon who considered the hearing a bothersome nuisance, he looked up and smiled at her when her briefcase came to rest beside his on the table.

"I can think of at least a hundred different places I'd rather be than here listening to these nature lovers complain about all the money this project will be bringing into the state. Can't you?" he asked in a low tone of voice, obviously not wanting the protesters behind them to overhear.

Leslie shrugged and took the seat beside him. "It's still a free country, Nathan," she said, folding her hands in her lap, wishing the day was over and gone forever. She could feel her employer's puzzled stare as he tried to evaluate her changed point of view. The old Leslie Rothe would have been angry and punishing to anyone who questioned the rightness of her reports or her final recommendations. The old Leslie was a gung ho, get-it-done girl. She'd had little tolerance for the opinions of others once she was certain she was correct in her own mind.

Jack Sullivan was the last to arrive. He took his place among the four other high-level forest-service officials at a long table facing the two dissenting parties. Jack and Leslie had worked together often over the years. They had developed a friendly rapport and respected each other's opinions. Rarely had they sat on opposite sides of an issue, and Leslie felt quite certain that if she spoke, Jack would listen attentively.

He read aloud the formal proposal submitted by Darby Development Company and touched briefly on the complaint submitted by the environmentalists, then he asked them to present their cases. Nathan's was short and sweet, outlining the project and the state revenue estimates projected to the year 2010. He frequently made reference to the report compiled and submitted by Leslie Rothe, and every time her name was mentioned she shuddered with shame and cringed with regret as she felt Joe's gaze boring into her from somewhere behind her.

When it was their opponents' turn to plead their case, Joe's own report was touched upon briefly, and they had just as many facts and figures to back up their arguments as Leslie had gathered for hers. But most of their data came straight from the heart. One impassioned plea after another was made. The protesters wanting the ski resorts and park lands confined to those areas already in use and to the periphery of the mountain range and the wilderness in the heart of the Colorado Rockies left as a gift to future generations.

As noon approached, there were still several more speakers to be heard on behalf of the environmentalists. A recess was called, and the hearing was adjourned for lunch. Leslie declined Nathan's offer to share the next ninety minutes together. She found herself to be poor company these days and already was feeling short tempered with him because of her own guilt. She wanted to be alone.

Filing out behind an orderly group of protesters, she kept her eyes lowered, afraid they would chance to meet a pair of sharp green ones that would instantly see the pain and misery she was harboring deep within her. Deception was never to be her ally, it seemed. Two feet outside the chamber doors, Joe stepped out in front of her, impeding her escape.

"Hi," he said, his voice low and tentative.

"Hi," she said, torn between self-righteous anger

and the pain of his rejection and the condemnation she felt for her own actions. She could hardly bring herself to look him in the eye. Her throat was tight, and the air was warm and thick. She could barely breathe.

"Are you well now? No problems from the snake-bite?"

"I'm fine. Thanks." She stepped out to go around him, but he reached out and took her arm to stop her.

"Leslie. I want to apologize."

"For what?" she asked, her confusion giving her the courage to look at him.

Joe looked around to make sure they were as alone as possible in the crowded corridor, then turned back to study her face in detail. "I shouldn't have left that note the way I did. I should have faced you, called an end to it face-to-face. But I wasn't sure I could. I'm sorry for that and, well, I'm sorry things didn't work out. I should have called for help that first night, I guess."

Leslie observed the tips of her shoes for several seconds, allowing him to finish while she tried to rein in her temper. It was a futile effort. "Mr. Bonner. If you've stopped me just to put an end to our affair for a second time, I can assure you, I got the message the first time. I don't appreciate your wasting my time in this manner."

"It wasn't a waste of time, Leslie. Not the time we spent in the mountains together. It just wouldn't work between us now. I'm not sure I could trust you again."

"Fine." This time she half pushed him out of her way so she could leave, although it was hard to tell where she was going. Tears blinded her, and her mind was a jumble of broken dreams and despair. She got a good ten yards away before she was overcome by one of those weird impulses that being in love seemed to produce in her. She turned back around and in an unLeslielike voice shouted down the hall, "You know, Joe Bonner, I hope that if you ever make a mistake, you remember to punish yourself as severely as you punish others for theirs. Maybe then you'll know what it's like to be human, and you'll realize what you're throwing away now."

The hearing resumed precisely at one-thirty. Leslie had met up with Nathan in the hallway and had used him as protection against another run-in with Joe. She found that his company hadn't been necessary. She didn't see Joe on her way back into the conference room. And once inside, she didn't bother to look to see if he had returned. She didn't care if he was there or not. And she kept on telling herself that, until a very interesting speaker rose to address the review board.

The woman, Ruth Collins, was tall and thin with a long, lean face. Her skin was darkly tanned by the sun as if she'd spent many hours out-of-doors.

"Mr. Sullivan, I'd like to bring to this board's attention the problem of the American bald eagle as a vanishing species in this country. It has been brought to my attention by a reliable source that there is a pair of eagles nesting in the area Darby Development plans to destroy. I can't believe that this board, in good conscience, would risk the loss of these severely endangered birds for any amount of money."

Jack Sullivan was frowning. His gaze met Leslie's. "I'm sorry," he said, with genuine concern. "I don't recall any mention in your report of eagles in the area, Ms. Rothe. Were you aware of this?"

"No, I wasn't aware of their existence at the time I filed the report. However, I, too, have recently received this information. I understand this is their second year in the same nesting place."

Jack was thoughtful for several seconds, then he again turned to Leslie. "In the past, under circumstances such as these, the developers have made provisions for the birds, building around them and giving them a great deal of space until they migrate and build elsewhere. Does this seem like a possibility in this case?"

"I'm sure my company would agree to that. However, I believe a special situation exists here in that the eagles have built their nest at a remarkably lower altitude than they usually choose. There may or may not be a reason. I'm not an eagle expert, and the information hasn't been available long enough to give it proper consideration."

Jack's eyes narrowed as he considered her words. Leslie knew him well enough to know that he felt her misgivings. But he apparently wanted to make sure he was guessing her intentions correctly as he rephrased his question. "Ms. Rothe, do you feel the birds would be safe if Darby Development proceeded with their plans, provided they make the usual concessions for the eagles?"

"I'm hardly the person to ask, Mr. Sullivan," she said, ignoring Nathan's elbow as it dug into her ribs. "The forest service, I think, would be a better judge of that. If you feel the change in nesting habits is insignificant and want to take the chance that developing the area won't produce some long-term effect on the eagles, then that's your choice. As I said, I'm not an expert in this field."

Jack and his colleagues discussed the matter for what seemed like a long time. When they finished, Jack once again gave Leslie a calculating glance before he spoke. "The project under consideration by Darby Development Company is one we had hoped would benefit both the private investors and the state. However, as an endangered species, the eagles must take precedence. We are fully aware that over the past few years their numbers have increased, but they're not out of the woods yet, so to speak. Like Ms. Rothe, none of us here," he indicated the other members of the panel, "is a trained ornithologist or eagle expert. We plan to file a recommendation that further investigation be made into this case, and the project's impact on the nesting eagles be fully evaluated. It is our opinion, since the leases have already been granted, that if the two parties here today cannot come to an equitable agreement, this matter should be taken up in the federal court of this district. We would like to thank all those who came today for their concern and honest opinions."

A loud din broke out in the room. Chairs scraped against the floor as people began to make their way out. Leslie and Nathan sat side by side, wordlessly, until the clamor had died down enough for them to speak.

"Why'd you do it, Leslie?" Nathan asked quietly. "If you'd have given Jack the go ahead, he would have agreed with you. He knows you're honest, and he trusts you. Why'd you warn him off?"

"Because I am honest and because he does trust me. And I want him to keep on trusting me."

"But those stupid birds aren't that big a deal, and you know it. You've changed your mind about the whole project, and I want to know why."

"Because it's wrong, Nathan. Have you been up there? Up to the project site?"

"Yes."

"You mean you've seen how beautiful it is, how untouched and irreplaceable it is, and you still want to build a ski resort in the middle of it?" She couldn't believe it. She had forgiven herself for her error, because she hadn't truly been cognizant of what she was doing. But she'd also vowed never to make that mistake again, no matter how busy she was or how much she wanted a project to succeed.

"A deal's a deal and money's money, Leslie. You know that. Where has this sudden attack of nature loving come from?"

Leslie thought about it. It hadn't come from Joe. She'd been heartsick about her judgment before she met him. It had come from her. She'd known about beauty and love long before she fell in love with Joe. She'd just never paid any attention to it. She'd taken it for granted. She hadn't seen the beauty of the land because it was always there and she had assumed it always would be. She hadn't paid any attention to love, because she'd always had it and was arrogant enough to believe she always would. Her family, her friends, and her fair share of men had loved her, and she'd taken their affection as her due. Being loved was as common and natural to her as breathing, and that's why she hadn't seen it.

It was the love she thought she couldn't have, Joe's love, that stirred and excited her. She'd never been rejected or without love before. She hadn't valued what she'd had or even been aware of it until she didn't have it anymore.

"It came from me. It was there all along, Nathan. I just didn't know it," she answered finally. She opened her briefcase and pulled out a plain white envelope. "Now that I do, I want to give this to you."

"What is it?"

"My resignation. I can't work for you and be truthful with myself at the same time. And I think I should warn you that this isn't the last you'll be seeing of me. I'm going to work on the other side of the fence. I'll be fighting you with all the energy I used to give to you, to keep you from destroying any more of our public lands."

"Are you crazy? You'll lose everything. There's no money in being noble."

"I know."

Logically Leslie's next move was to find a new job. She and the Department of the Interior had never been on the best of terms, but she knew they respected her work and considered her a formidable adversary. They might be willing to work with her as opposed to against her for a while, she calculated wisely. Of course, there was always the Environmental Protection Agency. She hadn't completely lost her mind. There were other jobs for research analysts that paid more, and she could always volunteer her time to the preservation of natural resources. At the moment, however, she didn't have the energy to decide what to have for dinner.

The review hearing that morning and her confrontation with Joe had taken their toll on what strength she had regained after her ordeal with the snake. The antivenin's side effects had left her drained and weak for days. Together with the agony in her heart, she had almost come to wish the snake had killed her after all.

But with the return of her strength had come a faith that perhaps with time, Joe would come to understand and try to forgive her. That last thread of hope had been dashed to the ground that morning, and she felt lower than ever. A sort of miserable lethargy consumed her. All she had the motivation for, all she wanted to do, was to mourn her love. She wanted to recall what was and dream about what might have been. She wanted to be alone with her fantasies of a happily ever after.

When the phone rang, she switched on the answering machine and turned the sound down so she wouldn't have to listen to the message. She took off her linen suit and left it on the floor where she'd dropped it. Wrapped in a soft terry robe, she made herself a cup of tea and settled herself in the chaise longue on her small balcony to watch the stars come out as the sun nestled into the mountains. The same stars had twinkled brightly and then faded in the dawn the night she and Joe had first made love. She drew in a deep breath and pretended to be able to smell the mountain pines. She listened for the rustle of leaves and the scuttling noises of small animals. . . .

She heard her door bell ringing. She tried to ignore it as her mind strove to regain that sense of happiness and contentment she'd had in the mountains with Joe. The gentle pinging became muffled noises and then a hard thumping on her front door. She blocked them out, hoping the person would go away as her body relived the acute, throbbing need low in her abdomen and the ecstatic anticipation at the tip of every nerve ending that Joe's touch had brought her. She ached to be close to him.

"Leslie." Her name wafted upward on the breeze from the street below. "Leslie. I know you're there. Answer me."

Joe's voice wasn't hard to recognize nor was the anxiety that riddled it. She sat up and looked over the railing at him. It seemed strange to see him in a suit. He'd probably had it on at the hearing, but she hadn't paid any attention to it. Even from a downward angle, his shoulders looked broader under the clean cut of his jacket, and his legs seemed to take on more mass when the finer material of his slacks replaced his jeans. He'd gotten a haircut too. Unwillingly and in absolute defeat, she had to admit her feelings toward him hadn't changed. It was one thing for her heart to ache and want to remember, but her brain had wanted to hate him. The fact that hating him was an impossibility, left a sour taste in her mouth and put a cutting edge on her words. "Now what do you want? To make sure I don't ever try to contact you again? You have my solemn vow."

"Come down and open the door, Leslie. We need to talk," Joe called back. His tone was less apprehensive and held that irritating note of authority he'd used when they'd first met.

What was he mad about now, she wondered. She'd done her best to correct her mistake, and he had gotten her out of his life. So where did he get off acting as if he had the slightest bit of influence over her anymore? "We have talked. Go away, Mr. Bonner."

"Don't call me that," he said, irritated. "I'm not a stranger. You know me better than anyone else in your life. And I know you better than anyone else in the world. Now, come down and open the door."

"No."

"What I have to say is private, but I'll shout it so the whole neighborhood can hear if you want me to," he threatened. Even though his attitude seemed somehow softer and more cajoling, she knew he was serious. He was determined to be heard, one way or another.

Suddenly it was all too much for Leslie to cope with. Her anger wasn't mighty enough to fortify her facade of casual disinterest. She did her best to swallow the painful lump in her throat, but it stayed and her words came out weakly. "Joe, please. Haven't we hurt each other enough? I'm sorry I didn't tell you the truth. I didn't mean to lie. I tried to tell you. I just didn't know how. I'm sorry about the mountain too. I don't even have a good excuse for that, so I won't offer you one. Can't we just let it go at that?"

"No." Leslie could hardly hear him, his voice was so low. "Come down and open the door. Please, Leslie."

She flopped back onto the longue and sighed. There didn't seem to be any way around it. Joe had come to say his piece, and nothing would deter him. She might as well get it over with, she determined, throwing her legs off the chaise, standing slowly so Joe could see that she was on her way down to the door.

When she opened the door to him, he was leaning with both hands on the door jamb as if eager to get in. His presence loomed over her. Her heart flipped over and began to beat vigorously despite her brain's warning that its excitement was in vain.

Joe studied her thoroughly for a second or two then scanned the room behind her before asking, "May I come in?"

"By all means," she said, with a wave of her arm. As long as he'd come this far, he might as well come in to pour salt in her wounds, she thought, relying on sarcasm as a buffer for what she knew was bound to be a traumatic ordeal.

He continued to look around her home with interest. Slowly he walked to the center of her living room, taking in her Chinese art collection, the wall of book-lined shelves, her wheat-and-brown-tweed modular furniture, and the electronic equipment she had amassed.

"Well, I can see why you weren't exactly *at home* up at the cabin," he said. Mild humor curled the corners of his lips and echoed in his hollow words.

Leslie had never seen Joe look so awkward. His gaze was actively seeking a place to rest, but resisted any temptation to come to light on her. His hands were shoved deep into his pockets, and Leslie frowned as he began to shift his weight nervously from one foot to the other. This wasn't the cocky, arrogant Joe Bonner she knew. This Joe Bonner was very worried about something. Like a homing pigeon, her heart went out to him.

"Would you like a drink or something?" she asked, and then wondered why she had. She wanted to be bitter and vengeful. She didn't want to care about him.

"Thanks, but I came here to tell you something, and I think I just ought to say it."

"Okay." Her voice was calm even as she spread her feet and braced herself for whatever was coming. She stood straight and immobile, but she felt as if she were a fragile porcelain doll. One more ounce of pressure, and she'd shatter into a million pieces. "Shoot."

Joe cleared his throat and glanced at her briefly, still unable to face her directly. "I'm not very good at making apologies. Not real ones. Not the kind you make when you're begging for forgiveness, when you want whatever has happened to be forgotten so that things can go on as if it never happened at all." He was silent for a moment. He examined the pattern in her rug for several seconds, then looked up, his eyes full of remorse. His gaze locked with hers. "I'm that kind of sorry, Leslie. I know I've hurt you, and you have every right to be mad, but I was hoping you might be able to forgive me."

He might as well have been speaking Latin for all Leslie understood of his impassioned speech. None of it made sense. He was the betrayed, she was the betrayer, right? "I don't understand," she admitted finally.

Joe took two steps toward her then appeared to stop himself from getting any closer. "You were right. This morning at the hearing, you were right. You made a mistake, and then I made a bigger mistake. And I was a hell of a lot harder on you than I was on myself. You should have told me about your job. I don't know why you couldn't bring yourself to tell me, but the more I thought about it, the more convinced I became that there must have been a good reason, because you've never been dishonest with me before. Maybe you didn't know me well enough to trust in my love for you, I don't know." He shrugged, and there was a look of sadness on his face as if he thought he had failed her somehow.

"But my mistake was in not giving you the chance to explain yourself. I was so bent out of shape because you hadn't told me and so afraid that I'd gotten involved with another liar that I didn't even give you a chance to tell your side of it. All I could think of was putting as much distance between us as possible so I wouldn't be hurt again. But it didn't work. I *was* hurt, and I missed you. I thought about you constantly. It wasn't until this afternoon that I realized I'd judged you on the merits of another woman. A dishonest, deceitful woman who wouldn't know the truth if it slapped her in the face. You aren't anything like her, Leslie. You never were. You were always honest with me. Brutally so," he said with a soft laugh. Then he sobered and asked, "Can you forgive me? Or is it too late?"

A fleeting impulse to teach Joe Bonner a good lesson raced through Leslie's mind. She might never again see him so low or so humble. But it was this same humility in him that reached her heart, and she instantly forgave him. "I haven't had a whole lot of experience, but I don't think it's ever too late if you love someone," she said.

Joe crossed the room in three long strides and took her hands in his. He looked deep into her eyes as if he couldn't believe that getting her to forgive him was truly so easy. When he saw that it was, his gaze softened and the familiar expression of loving adoration eased the lines of tension and concern in his face. He cupped the side of her face with his hand as if she were the most precious thing he'd ever touched. His voice was thick and deep when he spoke. "I really am sorry, Les. The last three weeks have been hell. And then when I discovered how stupid I'd been, I was so afraid that I'd lost you forever. I can't tell you how good it feels to be close to you again."

"You don't have to. I know. I've felt so empty inside." Leslie pressed her forehead to his shirt front, as if trying to transmit her thoughts and emotions directly through his chest wall and into his heart. "I wanted to tell you, Joe. I was so scared that you'd be angry, that it would ruin all the happiness between us. I thought we had more time. I kept hoping the perfect opportunity would come along to make it easier to tell you. I knew you'd be disappointed in me."

Joe sighed and wrapped his arms around her tightly. "I wish I could tell you that wouldn't have happened. But it probably would have. I have a lousy temper, no doubt about that. But once I've exploded, it's over, and I don't stay mad for very long, honey. Honest. I would have come around, and we could have talked it out. I value honesty like yours. Even when I'm angry, I recognize the courage it takes to tell the truth."

"Are you as good at making deals as you are at taking bets?" she asked, her eyes closed as she delighted in his embrace. It was like coming home and finding everything was the same. The familiar smells and sounds and sensations were right where she'd left them, in Joe's arms.

"I think so."

"Then I'll promise always to tell you the truth and face your anger, if you'll promise always to come back and let me explain."

Joe's laughter rumbled in her ear, and he squeezed her a little harder. "It's a deal." He pulled away slightly. Looking down at her, his face was animated with joy and merriment. "Is this where we get to kiss and make up?"

Leslie gave him a lazy, knowing smile. Her fingers deftly loosened the knot in his tie as she spoke. "We could do that. In fact, we could do that and then some."

The kiss they shared was a slow, deliberate act. It was more than a seal on a deal. It was a mutual vow to cherish the love between them, to nurture it, to strengthen it against the pressures of the world and protect it from their own faults.

Now Leslie had witnessed both sides of love. She had been loved and had taken it for granted, and she had been without love. She much preferred being in love, aware and susceptible to its every inclination. She felt tuned into Joe. He was a man who was bright and intelligent, a man who excited her and cared about who and what she was. A man, not perfect, with at least as many faults as virtues, but also a man who suited her, fit her like a glove, and balanced her life.

They had come too close to turning their backs on a love so great and perfect that it had been destined to be right from the start. Whether they had wanted it or not, it was bound to happen.

Joe moaned and ended the kiss, although he didn't release the hold that kept her as close as two clothed bodies could get. Nor did he restrain his hands as they wandered with familiarity over the body that he knew was his to possess. "Mm. I've missed those kisses of yours. Have I ever told you what a great kisser you are?"

"No. I don't recall that you have," she said. Her hands made their way along his strong, corded chest to the buttons that dotted the front of his shirt. "Is there anything else you've forgotten to tell me?" she asked, working at the buttons, fishing for the words Joe found hardest to say aloud.

"Not unless it's that I think you're pretty amazing."

"Me? Amazing? In what way?"

"Well, you could have knocked me over with a feather this afternoon when you and Ruth Collins pulled that eagle-out-of-the-hat trick."

"What makes you think I had anything to do with that?" she asked, trying to sound casual when she was actually worried that Ruth had broken her promise to keep her source anonymous.

"Because aside from the ranger, who obviously hadn't reported the birds, there were only two other people in the world who knew those eagles were there. And since one of them hadn't considered the birds as a possible deterrent, that left you."

"Now I'm amazed," she said, pulling away slightly to lead him to the stairs that went up to her bedroom. "You're a very clever man, Joe Bonner."

"I know. That's how I also figured out why you're no longer working for Darby Development."

With her mind elsewhere, Leslie wasn't prepared for all of Joe's cleverness. She came to a halt with one foot on the bottom step and stared at him in true astonishment. "How did you know that?"

"I'm a very clever man, remember?" he said, moving her along with him as he started up the steps. "I went there this afternoon looking for you. Imagine my surprise when they told me that you'd quit."

"Imagine mine when I decided to," she muttered, more to herself than Joe, as she recalled that day in

the hospital when she determined that if her life
was to be the way she wanted it, she would have to
make some changes.

"I hope you won't regret it. I wouldn't have asked
you to give up your job. Even though Darby Development operates at the polar negative to everything I
believe in, we could have worked something out so
we wouldn't have been constantly fighting, you know."

"Wait a second, Joe," she said, turning on the
step above him to look him straight in the eye. "I
love you, and I'd do almost anything you asked of
me. But I don't want you to get the wrong impression. I'd like to say that I quit my job and conspired
with Ruth Collins to get the project thrown into the
district courts for you. But the truth is, I didn't. I
wasn't sure I'd ever see you again when I made those
decisions. I made them for purely selfish reasons.
Getting the ski-resort project into the courts was
the only way I could make up for what I had done in
my ignorance. And you know that going to court
isn't a guarantee that the project will be stopped. It
all depends on the judge and whether or not he eats
Grape Nuts or Frosted Flakes for breakfast." She
turned, and they continued their ascent up the stairs
in the most natural way, hardly aware of where they
were going. Knowing only that their paths and their
destinations were the same, logged on the same
map for all time.

"As for my job, well, I think that was pretty much
over the minute I saw the mountain. I never would
have been able to do a good job for Darby and live
with myself after that anyway." She glanced up at
Joe. "Are you very disappointed that I didn't do it for
you?"

Joe smiled. His eyes were warm but quite serious
when he shook his head and answered. "No. Not at
all. I'm very proud of you. And I love you very much."

"What?"

"I said, I love you very much."

"Say it again, please."

Again Joe smiled. This time his gladness shone in his eyes. They had reached the top of the stairs. He made a quick perusal of his surroundings as his hands reached out and took hold of the sash on her robe. Apparently having found what he was looking for, he turned his full and undivided attention back on Leslie. The expression on his face sent chills of delight racing up and down her spine.

"I . . . love . . . you," he said, his voice a deep, stoking caress that coiled the muscles low in Leslie's abdomen. "I . . . love . . . you," he repeated, advancing on her, forcing her to walk backward in the direction he wanted to go, step by carefully calculated step. "I . . . love . . . you," he said again, releasing the sash and following her into the bedroom. "I . . . love . . . you." The robe slid from her shoulders and landed in a heap on the floor. "I . . . love . . . you."

THE EDITOR'S CORNER

I feel envious of you. I wish I could look forward to reading next month's LOVESWEPTs for the first time! How I would love to sit back on a succession of the fine spring days coming up and read these six novels. They are just great and were loads of fun for us here to work on.

Starting off not with a bang but an *explosion,* we have the first novel in *The Pearls of Sharah* trilogy, **LEAH'S STORY,** LOVESWEPT #330, by Fayrene Preston. When Zarah, an old gypsy woman, gave her the wondrous string of creamy pearls, promising that a man with cinnamon-colored hair would enter her life and magic would follow, Leah insisted she didn't believe in such pretty illusions. But when handsome Stephen Tanner appeared that night at the carnival, she saw her destiny in his dark eyes and fiery hair. He found her fascinating, beautiful, an enchantress whose gypsy lips had never known passion until the fire of his kisses made her tremble and their sweetness made her melt. Leah had never fit in anywhere but with the gypsies, and she feared Stephen would abandon her as her parents had. Could he teach her she was worthy of his love, that the magic was in her, not the mysterious pearls? Do remember that this marvelous book is also available in hardcover from Doubleday.

Unforgettable Rylan Quaid and Maggie McSwain, that fantastic couple you met in **RUMOR HAS IT,** get their own love story next month in Tami Hoag's **MAN OF HER DREAMS,** LOVESWEPT #331. When Rylan proposes to Maggie at his sister's wedding, joy and fierce disappointment war in her heart. She has loved him forever, wants him desperately. But could he really be such a clod that he would suggest it was time he settled down, and she might as well be the one he did it with? Maggie has to loosen the reins he holds on his passion, teach Ry that he has love to give—and that she is the one great love of his life. Ry figures he's going to win the darling Maggie by showing he's immune to her sizzling charms. . . . This is a love story as heartwarming as it is hot!

From first to last you'll be breathless with laughter and a tear or two as you revel in Joan Elliott Pickart's **HOLLY'S**

(continued)

HOPE, LOVESWEPT #332. Holly Chambers was so beautiful . . . but she appeared to be dead! Justin Hope, shocked at the sight of bodies lying everywhere, couldn't imagine what disaster had befallen the pretty Wisconsin town or how he could help the lovely woman lying so pale and limp on the grass. When mouth-to-mouth resuscitation turned into a kiss full of yearning and heat, Justin felt his spirits soar. He stayed in town and his relationship with Holly only crackled more and warmed more with each passing day. But he called the world his oyster, while Holly led a safe life in her little hometown. Was love powerful enough to change Justin's dreams and to transform Holly, who had stopped believing in happily-ever-after? The answer is pure delight.

Next, we have the thrilling **FIRE AND ICE,** LOVE-SWEPT #333, from the pen—oops—word processor of talented Patt Bucheister. Lauren McLean may look serene, even ice-princess reserved, but on the inside she is full of fiery passion for John Zachary, her boss, her unrequited love . . . the man who has scarcely noticed her during the two or three years she has worked for him. When John unexpectedly gains custody of his young daughter, it is Lauren to the rescue of the adorable child as well as the beleaguered (and adorable!) father. Starved for ecstasy, Lauren wants John more than her next breath . . . and he is wild about her. But she knows far too much about the pain of losing the people she's become attached to. When John melts the icy barriers that keep Lauren remote, the outpouring of passion's fire will have you turning the pages as if they might scorch your fingers.

There's real truth-in-titling in Barbara Boswell's **SIMPLY IRRESISTIBLE,** LOVESWEPT #334, because it *is* a simply irresistibly marvelous romance. I'm sure you really won't be able to put it down. Surgeon Jason Fletcher, the hospital heartbreaker to whom Barbara has previously introduced you, is a gorgeously virile playboy with no scruples . . . until he steps in to protect Laura Novak from a hotshot young doctor. Suddenly Jason—the man who has always prided himself on not having a possessive bone in his body—feels jealous and protective of Laura. Laura's pulse races with excitement when he claims her, but when a near accident shatters her com-

(continued)

posure and forces long-buried emotions to the surface, grief and fury are transformed into wild passion. Danger lurks for Jason in Laura's surrender though, because she is the first woman he has wanted to keep close. And he grows desperate to keep his distance! Jason has always got what he wanted, but Laura has to make him admit he wishes for love.

We close out our remarkable month with one of the most poignant romances we've published, **MERMAID, LOVESWEPT #335**, by Judy Gill. In my judgment this story ranks right up there with Dorothy Garlock's beautiful **A LOVE FOR ALL TIME, LOVESWEPT #6**. Mark Forsythe knew it was impossible, an illusion—he'd caught a golden-haired mermaid on his fishing line! But Gillian Lockstead was deliciously real, a woman of sweet mystery who filled him with a joy he'd forgotten existed. When Gillian gazed up at her handsome rescuer, she sensed he was a man worth waiting for; when Mark kissed her, she was truly caught—and he was enchanted by the magic in her sea-green eyes. Both had children they were raising alone, both had lost spouses to tragedy. Even at first meeting, however, Gillian and Mark felt an unspoken kinship . . . and a potent desire that produced fireworks, and dreams shared. Gillian wanted Mark's love, but could she trust Mark with the truth and shed her mermaid's costume for the sanctuary of his arms? The answer to that question is so touching, so loving that it will make you feel wonderful for a long time to come.

Do let us hear from you!

Warm regards,

Carolyn Nichols

Carolyn Nichols
Editor
LOVESWEPT
Bantam Books
666 Fifth Avenue
New York, NY 10103